Free

Free

Hope on the High Seas

Book One

Careena Campbell

Free (Hope on the High Seas, Book One)

Format by Careena Campbell. Edited by Careena Campbell and April Campbell. This book was created and formatted in Microsoft Word. Body text is size ten Book Antiqua.

Cover illustration copyright 2021 by Careena Campbell. Swirl, frame, and paper images on cover from pixabay.com; used by provision of copyright laws.

This is a work of fiction. Though the settings and locations are based on fact, such as the Bay of Biscay and Spain, the island and corresponding tribe are fictitious. The characters, ship, and events are fictional, and any resemblance to real people or persons is purely coincidental.

Dedicated to my Heavenly Father, for
doing above all we could ask or think,
and for writing the sailing story that
inspired mine:

Jonah chapter one!

Table of Contents

Acknowledgements

I cannot believe how much support I received for this book. Every time that I try to add it all up, I'm left so grateful for all the undeserved love and encouragement that I've received. Even the times someone just said "Sure, I'll read it" made a difference.

First, I must thank my Lord Jesus. Without Him, I couldn't have gotten this far. I had no idea what an immense, absorbing project I was getting into when I started this book, but He did. My hope in His faithfulness is what kept me editing and typing when I was in the doldrums. The book you're holding has been an almost four-year labor of love. At times I felt like I was pouring my blood, sweat, and tears into this. The only reason I was able to do it is because He already poured out His blood, sweat, and tears for me. His grace has been sufficient in my many times of weakness!

Mom. You have been so selfless, giving up so many hours editing with me, and sitting down to hear revisions when there were about a million other things you could have been doing! This book would not be what it is if it weren't for you.

Garrett, for being my sailing chum and first mate (and asking endlessly about when you could read my book!).

Dad, for always being there to help me sort through the complicated stuff of teenage life. I'm proud to say you're still the man in my life!

Uncle Gary and Aunt Barb — my history advisors and two of my biggest supporters. Thank you for everything!

All the wonderful people who have listened to me talk about my book and/or offered to read it. It really does make a difference!

You, the reader. Thank you for picking up this book and reading it and opening your heart to what it has to say. I don't know how many faces these pages will see, but you are one of them. I pray it will strengthen your faith and remind you of the freedom you have in Christ. If you're not saved, let this book tell you of the freedom Christ is waiting to give you.

Lastly, I must again thank the Lord. I started with Him and I'm ending with Him. Without Him, this book would be empty. He is the thread that ties this book together. May all the praise for this book go to Him!

To God be the glory!

Careena

Author's Historical Notes

I have tried to be as historically accurate as reasonable in this story. I enjoyed making sure many of the tools and terms the sailors use are actual ones from the time period. (If you ever see a term or phrase you don't recognize, check out the nautical dictionary at the back of this book.) It is my hope and belief that when you have finished this story you will have not only grown in your faith but also learned about what, to me, is a fascinating era.

An observant reader familiar with this historical setting may note that I have taken some creative license. For example, some of the hymns Ruth sings in this book did not exist in the mid-1600s. However, for the sake of familiarity and their fittingness with the story, I have chosen to include them anyway.

While thieving pirates and sea warriors have often been portrayed as the heroes of the sea, I wanted to write a book with cargo sailors at its base. They are often overlooked, but they were there; bravely traversing through what were often treacherous seas — without being the troublemakers that pirates were! Often it is the unnoticed men who do the best work…or as in this story, the unnoticed young woman.

May this book build your faith as it has built mine!

Free

Chapter One

Stowaway

My God will hear me. Do not rejoice over me, O my
enemy. Though I fall I will rise.

(Micah 7:7b-8a NASB)

O   the deep, deep love of Jesus; vast, unmeasured,
boundless, free." 17-year-old Ruth sang
worshipfully, walking in solitude along the beach. There
was a slight limp to her walk because she had been born
with one of her legs slightly shorter than the other.

"Rolling as a mighty ocean in its fullness over
me," she continued, slowly breathing in the cool ocean
air with every note. The soft, squishy sand squeezed
between her toes as the water swept over her feet. The
morning breeze teased the wisps of hair that had
escaped her long brown braid. As she walked along, she
carried her Bible in her hand.

"Lord," she prayed with a thoughtful sigh, "if it
be Your will, please send me a mission and a place to
belong." Pondering the many changes she had faced, as
well as the solitary life she now lived, she added, "I've
had ever so many 'short-term, hour-long' missions, but
no one thing...no one 'home' to call my own."

The peace of God's creation swirled about her as
she prayed to her Master.

Turning aside from the beach, Ruth climbed a
tree and pulled off a piece of fruit. Despite her short leg,
over the years she had taught herself to become excellent
at climbing trees.

Eating her fruit, she looked out over the ocean and watched big ships slowly creep their way toward the harbor. Several smaller boats floated about off the shore. The sun's rays reflected off the crystal water, sparkling so magnificently that it was almost blinding to look at. Ruth smiled and began singing. "For the beauty of the earth…"

Meanwhile, on a nearby cargo ship, the morning was not so peaceful.

"Ugh! Well, *I* don't want to clean them," fumed First Mate Leonard.

Captain Edward looked at him. "Everyone is busy pulling the ship in," he said calmly.

"Hmph," muttered First Mate Leonard. "I didn't get to the position I'm in to walk on filthy floors one of the lower ranks could be dealing with." Grumbling, he went below deck.

Meanwhile, back on shore, Ruth had tired of watching the ships. She turned around in the crook of the tree and began reading her Bible. The morning passed by as she turned page after page.

The cargo ship gradually prepared to dock.

"You're not pulling us in straight!" First Mate Leonard roared to the steersman.

"Actually, we're dead-on, sir," replied the steersman.

Captain Edward quietly observed the conversation. First Mate Leonard swaggered away, and Captain Edward silently contemplated the position of the ship. Nodding to the steersman, he walked away.

The sun was high in the sky by the time the ship had finished docking, although clouds had begun gathering in the distance. The crew began unloading old cargo and loading new on board. Ruth stood on a dock on the edge of the harbor, mostly hidden in the shadow of a large palm tree. Her braid was now pinned up in a bun, neatly covered by a linen cap, or *coif*. Curiously she observed the action of the harbor. The men she was watching were speaking English to each other, so Ruth found them more interesting than the usual Spanish sailors that worked in the harbor.

Ruth looked down at her Bible, thinking about how grateful she was to have it. It was one of her few possessions, but by far the most valuable. Without it, she would not have such a strong foundation in God's Word.

Abruptly, Ruth's contented thoughts were interrupted. She glanced up, realizing that a group of sailors were coming her way. Ruth quickly turned to leave. As she turned, her short leg slipped off the dock's edge and she fell head-first into something hard. *Thunk.* Her thoughts stopped.

First Mate Leonard lumbered over to the barrels, giving orders to the men who were with him. He half-tossed a lid onto a rather large crate and groaned as he lifted it. With much effort, he carried it to over to the ship and into the cargo hold. Walking back up, he wiped sweat from his forehead. As he went to get more cargo, he noticed the filthy floors. "Ugh," he muttered to himself. "I wish I could get someone to take care of that. But we all have more *important* things to do." Grumbling, he meandered down the ramp.

Thirty minutes later, the ship was underway. First Mate Leonard and Captain Edward supervised the men as they made sure everything was in the proper position as the ship eased out from the dock. Soon they were sailing freely, out into the ocean.

Meanwhile, Ruth's foggy mind slowly began clearing. All around her was darkness. Everything was rocking slowly back and forth. Where in the world was she? She tried to straighten up, but there wasn't any room to move in, and she felt as if she were upside down. As she lay crumpled in these strange confines, she tried to figure out what was going on.

As her thoughts finally cleared, Ruth suddenly realized she was inside something. What was she in? A cage? Panicking, Ruth thrashed around as violently as she could. She felt a falling sensation as the wooden vessel fell over, dumping her onto a wooden floor. Ruth glanced at the barrel she was finally free of. Barrel! That must've been whatever she had fallen into when she had slipped off the dock! Looking around, instead of beach and sky, she saw wooden walls and endless shelves, crates, and barrels. Uh oh! Something had happened! Where was she? Why hadn't someone seen her? Had someone captured her on purpose, or was this a pure accident? Would she be in trouble if someone found her? She needed to get out of here!

Wait — where was her Bible? Had she lost her most precious possession? Ruth desperately felt around on the floor for it. She peered into the barrel and glimpsed a dark object inside it. Reaching into the barrel, she felt a wave of relief as her fingers brushed the smooth cover. Breathing a prayer of thanks, Ruth pulled her Bible out of the barrel and glanced around. Across the room, Ruth spotted a door. She stumbled to her feet and, holding her Bible tightly between both hands, raced out of the room.

Outside the door was a long, narrow hallway, flanked with wooden paneling. Ruth continued running as fast as her short leg would allow. She spotted daylight coming in through the ceiling down the hall. She was almost out of here!

Suddenly, a scraggly man appeared in a doorway. Wide-eyed, he gasped, then his face turned to a scowl. "Who are you?" he roared.

Ruth felt a lump catch in her throat as she leaped onto the stairs that went through the hole in the ceiling. She willed her shaking arms and lopsided feet to climb the rough rungs, even though she knew the man was close behind her.

"Oy, get back here!" shouted the man. "Stop that girl! Stowaway!"

Ruth's eyes burned with tears of fear as she hurried across the deck. Something was wrong. She wasn't supposed to be here.

"STOWAWAY!" yelled someone high up in the rigging.

What! Deck! Rigging! Oh, no! She was on a ship? Glancing around, the shore was nowhere in sight. Ruth's jaw dropped, and her heart sank. "I'm stuck here?" she cried.

"YOU!" roared a voice from behind. Ruth whipped around. An angry sailor towered over her. "What are *you* doing here?" he demanded, grabbing her arm in a grip so tight, it hurt. His breath was so strong she could almost taste it in her mouth.

"Ahh!" Ruth shrieked. "Don't hurt me! It was an accident! I slipped into a crate and got knocked unconscious!"

The sailor's frown didn't lessen one bit, nor did his hold on her. "You really expect me to believe that?"

Ruth looked at his angry, cold expression. "I suppose not," she sighed. "But please, sir! Let me GO!" She yanked her arm in desperation, trying to break free from his brutal grip. "It's not my fault! I somehow got put in here, and now —"

19

"Woah, woah, woah! What's going on here, Stephan?" At this firm but less harsh voice, Stephan let go of Ruth's arm. Ruth stumbled back turned to see Captain Edward. She realized he must be the captain because of his clothes. His waistcoat looked far less worn than Stephan's, and over one shoulder was slung a dark red cloak. As she examined his serious eyes, Ruth thought she glimpsed a touch of concern.

Meanwhile, Captain Edward looked over this peculiar show-up. Her clothes were old and worn and quite possibly several sizes too small. Her skirt was frayed to above her ankles, revealing worn stockings that hardly covered her otherwise bare feet. She was clearly destitute, but Captain Edward could tell she took at least some care of her appearance. Her hair was covered by the typical coif, even though numerous flyaways had escaped and danced around her flushed face. She had no coat, but she did wear a partlet for modesty. Whatever kind of background she had, this was *certainly* not your typical stowaway, Captain Edward thought. "Calm down," he told her. "Now what happened?"

"I fell into a crate and I must've gotten knocked unconscious," Ruth explained desperately. "When I woke up, I was here on this ship. Please, sir, please— would you take me back?"

"Sorry, mistress," said Stephan. "We're all at sea and trying to outrun a storm. Right, Captain Edward?"

Ruth couldn't believe it. Surely they could just take her back and then wait out the storm! She stared at Captain Edward, her eyes pleading. Captain Edward silently returned her stare. He looked to be the same age Ruth's father would be. His beard was less scraggly than the other sailors', and his dark, wavy hair blew into his face as he thought. He opened his mouth as if he were about to speak. Ruth held her breath, hoping he would correct the sailors and tell them to take her back.

Rather, he stopped and said nothing. But his quietness gave Ruth a little hope that maybe not everyone on this ship was so harsh and rough.

A loud *thud* shattered the somewhat still moment. Stomping up the stairs, another sailor quickly approached behind Ruth's back. "STOWAWAY!" he roared, grabbing her arm. Ruth's dropped her Bible.

"Leonard!" gasped one of the men.

"No!" Ruth gasped. "Please! I'm not a stowaway!"

"Well, what else are you, then?" Leonard snapped, releasing her from his grip. Ruth lost her balance and tumbled to the floor. "You sneak onto a ship without anyone knowing, so what other name is there for you?" Leonard continued.

Ruth sighed, thinking to herself: *I never wanted to be a stowaway. I'm just a girl who needs some help.* Your help, if only you would be willing to help me.

Leonard interrupted her thoughts. "No matter," he muttered, bending over, grabbing her arm and forcing her to her feet. "This will solve a problem which I have long been wanting a fix for."

Ruth's eyes widened further, and she glanced around at the others. Was this allowed? Could he treat her so harshly? And what *now* did he want from her?

Leonard pointed to the opening in the deck's floor. "Down the hatch!" he ordered. He then swung his pointed finger into her face. "I want this ship cleaned like it's never been before!"

Ruth peered around the finger in her face and stared in disbelief at this self-proclaimed task master. "Me?" she whispered.

"Yes, you!" Leonard continued. "Stowaways will pay their passage. Now get to it! I've given you enough instructions already."

Ruth hesitated. She glanced at Stephan and Captain Edward, hoping for different instructions, but they were silent. Tears spilled out of her eyes as she turned away and disappeared down the steps as hastily as she could.

Despite the unsteadiness of her leg and the incessant rocking motion of the ship, she pushed forward through the hall. Eventually, she found the cargo hold she had first been in. Ruth paused for a moment. Crouching in a dark corner, Ruth cried, momentarily too scared to move. "Oh, Lord," she prayed as the tears spilled down her cheeks, "what is happening? Are they really going to keep me here? Surely they'll let me go! I don't want to stay here!" she sobbed.

Meanwhile, back on the top deck, Augustus, the sailing master, charged over to Leonard and roared, "What did you do THAT for! You know what people are going to think of us if they find out we have a captive woman serving as a slave on board!"

"I don't care what people think of us. It's not like it was my fault," Leonard answered. "We'll keep her for cooking and cleaning, and no more."

"But still!" Alessio, another sailor, protested, flipping his black ponytail off his shoulder.

"You have to go back and set her free!" demanded Charles, a watchman.

"That's enough!" Leonard yelled. "Do you or don't you want to beat the storm?"

The men quieted. Charles began, "Yes, but—"

"Alright, then. We're finished." Leonard was ready to be done with this conversation.

"But you have to set her free once we come back!" Augustus persisted.

"Why?" contradicted Sean, the boatswain. "I won't mind having some cooking and cleaning at my disposal from someone who *has* to obey me!"

"Are you out of your mind?" gasped Alessio. "We can't possibly keep a trapped girl on board! We're cargo sailors, not pirates!"

Augustus narrowed his eyes at the men arguing to keep Ruth. "I'm beginning to think this mess is your fault. The only container with a lid that she could have fit in was that barrel Leonard got!"

"No. Honestly. I had nothing to do with it," Leonard said truthfully. "I didn't even look in that crate."

"Well, whose fault is it, then?" Charles growled.

Charles began pushing at Stephan. Augustus grabbed Leonard's shirt, and Leonard pulled back a fist to punch. Sean blew his whistle, and they all stopped. Captain Edward slowly walked to the center of the group. "Master, you'll release her once we come back?" Alessio pleaded.

Captain Edward opened his mouth to respond, but then he saw First Mate Leonard's scowl. He really didn't want to pick a fight with Leonard right now. Captain Edward sighed and with a nod to the other men, said, "We'll see."

Meanwhile, down below deck, Ruth wasn't sure how to move on, but she figured the sailors would be angry if she didn't get working. She rose to her feet, but her legs wobbled. Her initial adrenaline had worn off, and now her legs felt exhausted. Leaning on the wall for support, she slowly walked to a corner where she could see an old broom propped up against the wall. Ruth reached for the handle, and her nose turned up. It was old and nasty and caked with dirt. Gingerly she picked it up and stumbled out of the room.

Ruth tried to decide where to start. Slowly, she made her way down the corridor through the ship. She passed multiple small rooms. Just past what appeared to be a mess room she found herself in a compartment with a stove — probably the galley. Ruth glanced around the hall, then slipped into the small room. None of the sailors were doing anything in the galley right now, but she guessed that if it *was* in fact the galley, they did use it frequently. Perfect. A room where she could stay away from them and still be sweeping a place they would want cleaned.

Shaking her head in an attempt to keep back the tears, Ruth began sweeping. The dirt pile grew fast — it had obviously been a long time since anyone had cleaned this ship very thoroughly, but Ruth barely noticed. She was too overwhelmed with thoughts.

Why do You have me here? she asked God honestly. She bit her lip to try to keep from crying, but tears were already spilling out. *What am I supposed to do? What should I do if they* don't *let me go? Escape? But how would I? I'm so confused. Oh, God, help me!* Her thoughts swirled through her mind until a loud voice from the hall interrupted them.

Thankfully, she realized the sailor was talking to someone else, but the interruption made Ruth snap back to attention. For now, there was no time to think of a way to escape. She would just have to busy herself and hopefully keep the sailors happy with her. She looked at the large pile of dust and dirt at her feet. What would she use for a dustpan?

Her red, tear-filled eyes glanced around the room. She spied a small, cracked bucket and swept the pile into it.

Now where? The top deck probably needed it, but the sailors were up there. Ruth wouldn't dare be near them. They were making a lot of noise, and Ruth shuddered to think of being surrounded by whatever they were doing.

She reached a second cargo hold, but would the sailors want a storage room cleaned before the other rooms and halls? She settled for the hallway.

Now and then a sailor would brush past. Ruth tried not to look at them, hoping they weren't going to yell at her or rough her around. Except for an occasional frown, they mostly left her alone.

Despite the lump in her throat, Ruth found comfort in singing. Quietly, she mumbled, "O God, our help in ages past, our hope for years to come, our shelter from the stormy blast, and our eternal home…"

It was a long, long time before evening came. It felt like it was taking forever for the sailors to go to bed. Once they did, Ruth figured she could, too.

Finally, anxious Ruth noticed several of them heading, one by one, into their cabins. Ruth decided to look for her Bible before she went to bed, since she had lost it in the scuffle with the sailors. With a deep breath, she walked up to the top deck and looked around. She didn't see her Bible anywhere. She thought a moment, then walked over to where Captain Edward and Leonard were standing.

After a quick prayer, Ruth spoke up bravely: "Sir, do you know where my Bible is?"

Captain Edward looked at her and shook his head. "I don't remember seeing—"

"Yeah, I found it, but you shouldn't have left it on the deck," First Mate Leonard interrupted.

Ruth swallowed hard. She *really* wanted it back. Meekly, she ventured to ask another question: "May I please have it back, Master Leonard?"

"*First Mate* Leonard," Leonard corrected. "And no, I'm not going to get it right now. I have more important things to be doing."

Ruth hesitated, but she decided to persist would only get Leonard angry with her. "Alright," she swallowed. As she turned away, Ruth felt relieved they hadn't been upset with her for speaking up, but she desperately wanted her Bible back. She needed to find some sort of encouragement right now, and God's Word was the only place she knew she could get it. What if Leonard *never* found it "important" enough to give back to her? Pushing aside her troubled thoughts, she decided to try to find a place to sleep for the night. She decided to go back to the storage room she had first been in. Once she reached the room, she glanced around for a safe spot to sleep. In the corner, she spied a stack of sacks. She stumbled over and slumped onto them. Now hidden in the shadows and out of sight of the door, Ruth lay frozen, too exhausted to move. Afraid and confused, Ruth broke down and cried. This day had been so hard, and now she didn't know if there would be any relief tomorrow.

As her red eyes glanced wearily around the room, Ruth spied something small and black lying on the floor nearby—something that resembled the shape of book. But how could it be? Pulling herself off the sacks, she grabbed it. Yes, praise the Lord! It was a Bible.

Ruth blew the dust off the cover and began flipping through the epistles. "I *know* I've read a verse about servants," she decided. She passed Romans, the Corinthians, and Galatians before landing in Ephesians.

"Here it is," she said, looking at chapter six verses five through eight. "'Servants, be obedient to them that are *your* masters according to the flesh, with fear and trembling, in singleness of your heart, as unto Christ: not with eyeservice, as men-pleasers; but as servants of Christ, doing the will of God from the heart; with good will doing service, as to the Lord, and not to men: knowing that whatsoever good thing any man doeth, the same shall he receive of the Lord, whether *he be* bond or free.'"

Once again, Ruth sighed, tears falling onto the rough, scratchy sacks. "Oh, Lord, I always thought if I ever was put into a situation like this, I'd be the quiet heroine that was such a good example that everyone changes in the end. But this is HARD, and I don't think I can do it!" At that, Ruth stopped herself. "You wouldn't send me something I couldn't handle. But still, this is so hard!" Ruth continued praying to her Redeemer until she fell asleep.

Careena Campbell

Chapter Two

Trying Hard

I can do all things through Him who strengthens me.

(Philippians 4:13 NASB)

"Oy! You! Woman!" A loud voice and sudden knocking awakened Ruth. "Where are you hiding?"

Ruth groggily rolled over on the hard floor. She rubbed her eyes in an attempt to keep them from closing again. Ruth groaned. How could it possibly be time to get up already? "I'll be there in a minute!" she called. Feeling weak and sore from yesterday's ordeal, she rolled over again and grabbed her Bible. She knew the sailors wanted her to get working, but her relationship with God was more important. She sat up quickly and read a few verses.

"Lord," she prayed before heading out, "I need Your help to be brave and to speak wisely. I want to be a good servant, to them and to You. Help them see You in me. And please help me stay safe. Amen."

"Woman!" the voice called again. This time it was closer. "Shake a leg and get out here! You know better than to try and get out of your work, you stowaway!"

Ruth cringed, but she obediently rose to her feet. "Yes, sir, I'm coming!" she answered. She limped to the door and hesitated at the grumpy sailor before her. He had dark skin and a curly beard, and he wore a strip of fabric tied over his forehead. It probably served to help all the braids in taming his extremely curly hair. Hands on his hips, he wore an impatient expression as he frowned at Ruth.

"Finally," the sailor commented, and he turned to walk away. "You better not hide next time," he said over his shoulder.

"Sir," Ruth addressed him hesitantly.

"That's Master Sean to you," he corrected.

"Alright, Master Sean," Ruth answered respectfully. Inwardly, though, she was nervous about how nice Sean was going to be. "What would you like me to do today?"

Sean thought for several moments, but he couldn't think of anything specific. He shrugged. "Whatever needs doing."

Ruth took a deep breath as Sean walked away. *Thank you, Lord,* she thought. *That should make things easier.*

Ruth decided to continue sweeping. The men's quarters probably needed it, but she couldn't go in there while they were in it. That meant she needed to do the top deck.

"I guess I can't just avoid them all day," Ruth decided. "Lord, please give me courage."

Ruth bravely stepped up to the top deck and began sweeping a corner. "Good morning, Captain," she greeted.

Captain Edward nodded. "Good morning." He began to walk away, but momentarily turned back. "What's your name, miss?"

Ruth looked up from her broom. "Ruth," she replied. "Ruth Brett."

Captain Edward nodded. He then turned away and began talking with another sailor. "So, what were you saying earlier, Alan?"

Alan looked to be early twenties—maybe even a little younger than that. He pulled the sweatband off his head and ran his hand over his brown hair. "I was saying we neglected to get rid of that old dinghy."

"Oh." Captain Edward thought a moment. "I don't have a use for it."

"Well, none of us want that hulking thing, either!" Alan laughed.

Ruth looked over the side of the ship. A small wooden boat trailed beside the ship, tied to the ship by a rope.

Suddenly Ruth felt something brushing between her feet. "AHH!" she shrieked, pushing back from the railing. She lost her balance and fell over.

Laughter erupted behind her. She turned to see the sailors pointing and laughing at her.

"Oy, please!" Alan exclaimed. "Haven't you ever seen a rat before? That's ship life!"

Sean snickered and shook his head. "Landlubber," he muttered.

Ruth felt her face turn deep red. She swallowed hard. Of *course* she'd seen rats before. She couldn't help it of she got spooked if one ran right under her—or if her short leg made her off-balance! Standing up, she fought the tears welling in her eyes.

Captain Edward turned around from talking with one of the other men, wondering what all the ruckus was about. He looked at Ruth. He wore a disapproving look as he glanced over at the men, but he said nothing.

Ruth turned away, resumed sweeping, and kept her eyes rooted to the floor. She felt uncomfortable, like their penetrating eyes were still staring at her.

Scritch, scritch, swish. The broomstraws swirled across the wooden deck floor. Ruth swept the pile into the bucket. It was pretty much full now.

Ruth limped over to the captain and forced a smile. "Pardon me, Captain." She hoped he wouldn't laugh at the simple question she was about to ask.

"Aye?" Captain Edward answered.

"I was wondering what to do with this trash."

Captain Edward shrugged. "Dump it into the ocean."

Ruth looked confused. "Isn't that bad for God's creatures that live there?"

Captain Edward looked at her. "Not as bad as it would be if we had trash lying around."

· Ruth thought a moment. "Alright. In that case I guess I'd better do it."

As Ruth walked away, she heard Captain Edward behind her. "You're a Christian, aren't you?"

Ruth's whipped around, and her eyes lit up. "Yes, sir! Saved—saved by Jesus' blood."

Captain Edward smiled a tiny smile and walked away. Ruth took the bucket over to the edge of the ship. As she dumped it out, a voice bellowed behind her: "Oy, lass, aren't you going to make us dinner?"

Ruth whipped around. *Uh oh,* she thought. *I'm not that good of a cook.*

"Uh…" Ruth hesitated. "What do I make?"

"That's yours to figure out," the sailor instructed in a rather harsh tone.

"So...I build a fire?"

"NO!" the sailor gasped. "I mean yes, but only in the hearth. And be *very* careful—fire is a major hazard on a ship."

"Alright," Ruth answered, a little startled by his firmness.

Ruth walked to the galley. A few pieces of fruit lay on the counter, but other than that, the only food was in barrels.

Peering into the barrels, Ruth contemplated her options. "Well, I guess I could make pea soup. But I haven't made that in a really long time. I think I could do it. Well, I don't know. It's been so long since I cooked for other people," she sighed. "No doubt it won't taste as good as it could. What if they don't like it?"

Slowly, Ruth stumbled back up to the top deck. Not finding the captain, she walked back down, nearly crashing into him.

"Oh!" Ruth gasped. "I beg your pardon. Oh! Captain, may I ask a question?"

"Of course." Captain Edward stopped walking and turned toward her.

"Um..." Ruth began awkwardly. "So, I was going to make your dinner, but it might be awhile. I just wanted to make sure you don't want your men to make something themselves, because they might be able to do it quicker. But, if you don't mind a wait, I'd be more than willing to do it." Ruth shifted uncomfortably. It seemed an odd question to be asking the captain, but she considered him to be more even-tempered than the other sailors.

Captain Edward didn't seem to care. "I don't see any reason why they would do a better job than you would."

"Alright. Lord willing, hopefully, I'll have it ready somewhat soon." Ruth took off for the galley but had to stop and regain her balance.

Captain Edward seemed lost in thought as she took her leave.

In the galley, Ruth built a fire in the hearth, minding the sailor's warning to be careful. With much effort, she lifted the big black pot into place and dumped some ingredients into it.

As the fire heated up, Ruth looked around the room, analyzing what dishes there were. A knife lay on the table, and a platter sat on the floor with a spoon on top of it. Wooden plates and tin bowls were scattered here and there across the floor, and she assumed there must be more hiding somewhere in the room.

Ruth squinted her eyes. "Really?" she squeaked. "I have to find what I need in this mess?" Ruth sighed. "God, I guess I always thought that working with people would make life easier. But this seems like the opposite. These sailors have no idea what they're asking me to do. They want me to complete their wishes quickly, but they don't even have things where I can. Besides, people don't normally have *one* slave do *all* the work, right?" Ruth continued sorting through her confused thoughts as she added ingredients to her concoction. It sure looked strange right now. She hoped it would turn out alright.

Sean walked in, grabbed a piece of jerky, and shoved it into his mouth. "You almost done?"

Ruth looked down at the soup. It was simmering now, but it certainly was too watery to serve for a while yet. She dipped her spoon into the green liquid. "I'm not sure," she answered truthfully.

"Hurry it up, then," Sean answered bossily, taking his leave.

Ruth swallowed hard. *God,* she thought, *I think some of them are just* trying *to give me a hard time. I mean, help me not judge them, but it sure seems like that.*

Ruth stacked another log onto the fire. She watched the soup expectantly, hoping it was going to pick up its pace.

"This is just going to take way too long to have for dinner," Ruth sighed, feeling stressed. "I'm going to have to think of another plan." Working quickly, Ruth put some cheese and dried meat onto the tray and walked up to the top deck. She hovered nearby the sailors, who appeared to be having a conversation. Not wanting to interrupt, she waited a few feet away.

Finally, a sailor with long, black hair walked away from the group. He saw the girl with the tray.

"Want some?" Ruth blurted.

The sailor examined the tray. "What are they?"

"Meat and cheese," Ruth answered. She added nervously, "If it's not enough, I apologize. We were going to have soup, but it's not going to be ready for a while. I guess we'll have to have it for supper."

The sailor picked one up and crunched it, chewing with his mouth open.

Ruth waited for a response.

"That's fine," was all he said.

The other sailors turned and walked over. Ruth held out the tray to them. Her legs wobbled, and she hoped she wouldn't drop it.

"Aye, this is nice," chuckled a sailor, brushing crumbs off his beard. He looked at Ruth, and with a teasing tone he added, "Guess you're a keeper."

Ruth's eyes widened, and her stomach did a flop. Did that mean he liked her food or that he'd never set her free? She tried to push his comment out of her mind as she served the other sailors.

As they walked away, over walked Captain Edward. He fiddled with his hair as he picked up a piece of cheese.

"You know," he said, "you could have just asked me to have them figure out their own meals."

Ruth felt tears welling up in her eyes and found herself looking straight into his. She wanted to yell, "No I *didn't* have to do it!", but more than that she wanted to honor God. "Well," she began, swallowing hard, "one of you asked me to make a meal, and you're my authority. So, since it wasn't against God's Word, I needed to try to do it."

Captain Edward momentarily didn't respond. As he looked deep into Ruth's face, Ruth turned her eyes to the floor. She wondered if he cared enough to see the hurt that hid there. Captain Edward nodded before turning away. "Thank you, Mistress Ruth."

Ruth was slightly stunned. A small smile crept onto her face; perhaps from hearing her own name and from being appreciated. Perhaps because hearing her name reminded her of her parents.

At thinking about her parents, Ruth began feeling upset again. But she straightened herself upon seeing the only person she hadn't served yet: First Mate Leonard. Bravely she walked over to him.

"Pardon me, sir," she smiled. "May I offer you some of these?" As he picked one up, Ruth tried to hide

Free

her nervousness. He took a bite, then picked up a few more.

Ruth expected him to say something, but he didn't. Relieved, Ruth walked back to the galley. Maybe things were getting better... or at least she hoped so.

The afternoon passed much like the morning, and when the sailors demanded supper, Ruth decided to serve the soup. It wasn't as good as her mom's, but Ruth didn't know what else to add to it. How she wished her mother could be here to help her!

"One, two, three, four, five, six, seven, eight, nine, ten...twenty-three. I think that's enough bowls for everyone, including me. I hope the men like it alright. I'm not sure if meat went in my mom's soup. But at least I tried to ask them what they wanted." Ruth cringed. Earlier she had asked the men if meat normally went in pea soup.

"It's not our job to know that," First Mate Leonard had snapped. "You ought to know how to do those things!"

But I don't know how, Ruth thought sadly. *And why do they assume I would know how to do all that they ask? I mean, a lot of women would know to do these things, but I haven't had a chance to learn some of them. Oh Lord, I'm so confused. Maybe I really should try to escape.* Ruth wasn't sure how to face her future. What did God want her to do?

Ruth spooned soup into the last bowl. Up the stairs walked the hurting captive to call the men in for supper.

"Supper's ready," she said plainly.

"Finally," grumbled Sean. All the men filed into the small room beside the galley, except for the few who stayed above deck to man the ship.

37

The men sat around a central table on barrels, trunks, and whatever else was lying around. Ruth stood nearby, hoping nothing more would be said to her, but not sure they would want her to leave. As one of the sailors dunked his spoon into his bowl, he glanced over at Captain Edward before whispering, "Oy. Bring me some water, would you?"

"Oh. Of course. Uh…where is it?"

"In the cargo hold."

"Alright. I mean yes, sir." Ruth grabbed a tray and crept over to a small pile of mugs on the floor. She carefully picked them up and set on her tray. They were dusty, but Ruth had nothing to wash them with right now.

Slowly, slowly, Ruth walked to the cargo hold. The tin mugs jostled on the tray. Upon reaching the dusty, dirty room, she set the platter down. She shuffled around in the dark, filthy room looking for a water barrel. "How am I supposed to know which one it's in?" she wondered. But then she spotted several barrels of clear liquid.

"There they are." One by one, she filled each mug.

"Uh oh," she breathed as she picked up the wobbly tray. "I hope I don't drop this." She slowly took a step forward. The full cups slid and banged together and on the edge of the tray.

"This isn't a good idea," she resolved. She set the tray down on the floor and picked up a cup in each hand. Back to the mess room she walked.

Walking around the table, she placed one mug in front of Captain Edward and the other beside First Mate Leonard. "I'll go get the others," she informed them.

Free

"Mistress," Captain Edward called. "Thank you."

Ruth forced a weak smile. "My pleasure, captain."

Eventually, the men finished eating, and Ruth could finally retreat to her own room to eat *her* soup.

As evening fell, a tired Ruth decided to wash the dishes. She made her way to the cargo hold, bucket in hand. Peering into the water barrel, she mused, "I hope they have more of this. It'll be gone fast with me washing dishes." Ruth decided to only fill her bucket half full.

Ruth wanted to watch the sunset while she did her dishes, so she grabbed a few bowls before heading up to the top deck. The water in the heavy bucket sloshed back and forth as she stepped up the stairs.

First Mate Leonard spied her water-filled bucket. Suddenly, he realized where it must have come from. "No!" he gasped. He charged over to her. "You don't use drinking water for dishes!" he roared into her face. He yanked the bucket from her with such force that Ruth fell backward and landed on the deck—hard. "You need to learn how to be on a ship!" Leonard demanded.

As First Mate Leonard walked away, Ruth lay on the floor of the deck. She sat up, blinking back the big tears that were already welling up in her eyes. Hanging her head, she gently touched her foot. She had bent it the wrong way when Leonard knocked her over. Softly she stroked her bruised arm. Her body wasn't hurt badly, but her heart was. *That does it!* she thought as tears spilled down her cheeks. *I can't take any more of this!* Ruth rose to her feet and stumble-ran for the hatch.

Just before she reached the stairs, Captain Edward entered the scene. He immediately noticed

Ruth's face, and he looked concerned. "What happened? Did he hurt you?"

"It doesn't matter!" Ruth cried, racing away. Captain Edward couldn't undo the hurt Leonard had already caused her. All Ruth wanted was to get away and hide in the cargo hold.

Captain Edward glanced disapprovingly at First Mate Leonard, but he still said nothing.

Ruth slowed as she slid through the door to her room. She tumbled into the shadows and hid herself behind the stack

"What am I going to do?" she moaned. Her thoughts raced. "I was hoping that Leonard was going to get better. I gave him the benefit of the doubt. I thought maybe the way he treated me when we met was just random; that he wouldn't really be that way most of the time. I should've known better. But I was trying to be forgiving! This isn't fair, God! He's getting worse, not better! What's next? What will he do to me next time I mess up?" Ruth's eyes widened, her heart raced, and her hands trembled. Her mind whirled with the possibilities of what might happen—and how far he might go. "I'm not going to stick around to see. I'm getting out of here." Ruth thought of the dinghy trailing the ship. "*Tonight,*" she whispered.

Chapter Three

Risks

R uth lay curled up in the corner, her anxious eyes glancing about the dark room. What time was it? It seemed that she had been lying there forever. Not asleep, but waiting and wondering. But was it a problem that she hadn't been asleep? She was already worn out from the day's work, and now she was about to embark on a dangerous and risky adventure.

For the third time during the night, Ruth crept out of the room and tiptoed up the hallway. Up the stairs she crept, hoping each small creak wouldn't call someone's attention. Most of the sailors had long been asleep, but Ruth didn't know if she could escape the night watchman's notice.

Quietly, quietly, she tiptoed to where she could see the watchman up on his lookout. It was hard to tell in the darkness, but it looked like maybe he was resting. Scanning the deck, Ruth saw no one else around. Her eyes widened. This was the chance she had been waiting for. She glanced around and saw a rope sitting on top of a barrel. She tiptoed over to it and quietly picked it up. Then, as quietly as she could, Ruth walked over to the side of the ship where the dinghy was and tied the rope to the railing.

"Woah," Ruth breathed, peering over the edge. "It's a long way down." She lifted her short leg over the rail, but she couldn't get her other leg over without fearing that she'd lose her grip.

Ruth climbed back off the rails. This time, she tried swinging her longer leg over the rail first. *I'd better hurry up or he's going to see me!* she thought. Her whole body was stiff with anxiety. She swung her short leg over and found herself resting her feet on the edge of the ship.

She stood there staring downward for several moments. Then she carefully lowered herself until she was hanging off the side of the ship, hanging onto the rope with her hands and balancing her feet on the ship's side.

Her hands trembled. "I don't think I can do this!" she whispered. "If I fall and hit it the wrong way, it'll flip!" She hung there for several seconds, trying to make up her mind.

"I can't," she resolved, beginning to pull herself back up. But then she remembered what she was trying to protect herself from. "I can't risk being with them, either!" She made up her mind and let one hand off the rope. Then suddenly — *whoosh* — she slipped down the rope.

Ruth managed to grab ahold of the rope again and began lowering herself more carefully. She swung back and forth as she worked her way down the rope. Down, down, down Ruth climbed until she felt her foot brush the little wooden boat.

She let go of the rope and landed on the hard wood. Ruth looked up. The ship's edge was now high above her.

I did it! Ruth thought. *But I'd better hurry. I need to get out of here before they see me!* Fingers fumbling, Ruth unknotted the rope from the dinghy and found herself floating freely in the ocean. She began rowing away, away from the ship and off on a path of her own.

"I'm FREE!" Ruth rejoiced quietly. "Oh, thank You, Lord! I did it! Now for the rest of my plan. The first part was to escape on this boat, since the sailors don't want it. Part two is to get to that island." Ruth's eyes traced the outline of the dark shape on the moonlit horizon. "They sailors mentioned that there's a tribe there. They can help me."

Ruth continued rowing as she embarked on her adventure. Her heart swelled with the thrilling joy of being free.

.   .   .   .   .   .

Thirty minutes after Ruth's escape, it was a few hours before dawn. Ronan, the night watchman, started awake. What? Yikes! He had been sleeping? Hopefully no one had noticed, otherwise he was going to be in big trouble. He couldn't remember the last time he had fallen asleep on watch duty! He shook off his drowsiness and peered through the fog that had fallen. His eyes locked on a black mound floating above the southern horizon. Storm clouds!

Before Ronan's very eyes, the clouds crept toward the ship. There was no doubt the storm was going to catch up with them!

"ALL HANDS ON DECK!" Ronan yelled. "The storm is overtaking us!"

The other sailors came running up to the top deck. Sean, being the boatswain, gave a long blast to his whistle and began instructing the men how to adjust the sails. Captain Edward saw the dark clouds and immediately gave orders: "Leonard, you and Alessio stow the loose items up here. You three, get everything secured below deck. Stephan, batten down the hatches. Everyone else, up in the sails!"

The sailors sprang into action. The sails rolled up like giant blankets over the men's heads as they scrambled to secure the ship.

"Where's the girl?" wondered Sean. "She needs to be up here helping us!"

"I'll go get her!" offered Alan.

"No, you won't," Captain Edward interjected. "I will!" He raced down the stairs and glanced in every room. "Ruth! Ruth! Come quickly! A storm is coming!" He reached the final room, but he hadn't found her. "Mistress Brett?" Puzzled, he tried to think of where she could be.

"CAPTAIN!" yelled Augustus. "The dinghy is gone!"

Captain Edward's eyes filled with horror as he rushed up the stairs. He glanced over the side of the boat. Where the dinghy had once been, there was now only a rope, with a second hanging next to it. He groaned.

"NO!" he yelled. "Ronan! What happened? Why didn't you see her?"

Ronan's face turned red. "Well, I was, I was —"

Leonard gasped. "Don't tell me you were asleep!"

"I'll deal with you later," Captain Edward groaned. "Right now, we need to find her. That dinghy is damaged, and these waters are dangerous!" Captain Edward's face tightened.

Angrily he turned to the men. "How have you been treating her?" he demanded. He was met with silence.

"That's what I thought," he said. "Now, I order everyone to search urgently! Theodore, you get in the mizzen lookout and see if you can spot her. Alessio, you get on the foresail. NOW!"

The men flung into action, and Captain Edward turned back to the side where the lifeboat once was. *They scared her, so she thought she had to escape,* he thought

44

regretfully. *Alas! I hope she survives out there. If we don't find her soon, what are the chances she will survive?*

.   .   .   .   .   .

Ruth wasn't paying attention to the dark clouds on the horizon. She was focused intently on rowing. Her eyes glowed with happy determination as the oars slowly revolved around and around. Her legs might be weak, but her arms were strong. Joyfully she sang, "It is well, it is well with my soul!"

The wind seemed to join in her song as she ebbed her way toward the island. The potential dangers ahead never even crossed her mind.

.   .   .   .   .   .

Back on the ship, the sailors were frantically trying to spot their lost servant girl. The windspeeds were picking up, and the sea was beginning to churn.

"Captain," called Theodore, yelling over the chaos, "We can't spot her! This fog is too thick, and she might be too far!"

"Alas!" groaned Captain Edward. "We have to! There's no way she could possibly survive without our help!"

Captain Edward glanced out upon the tempestuous waters. *Storms here on the Bay of Biscay can grow terribly violent,* he thought. *She's in danger of being caught in this storm.* Another troubling thought crossed his mind. *But that's if her dinghy is still intact. Oh, no. If it springs a leak before we find her, she's not going to make it.* Captain Edward felt panic and guilt rise in his chest. *If Leonard would have just let the men take her back and wait out the storm, none of us would be in this danger.* Captain Edward sighed, running his fingers through his dark brown waves.

.   .   .   .   .   .

Out in her little rowboat, Ruth noticed that it was getting harder and harder to row. Her tiny ship boat was being rocked by the waves. Glancing behind her, Ruth looked through the haze and saw the threatening clouds. "Uh oh," she breathed. "I'd better hurry up!" She worked faster as raindrops began sprinkling around her. She was only a few yards from shore now, and before long she would be safe on the beach.

"Just a little further," she coaxed herself. Her arms ached, but after a two more rounds of the oars, the boat nosed into the sand.

"Huzzah!" Ruth cheered. She hopped out of the boat — *Splash, splash* — and pulled it onto the beach — *Slosh, slosh.*

"There," Ruth announced with a contented sigh. "Thank You, God! My plan is working!" Ruth set off to find the tribe as the raindrops made tiny ditches in the sand.

Slowly, carefully, Ruth inched through the jungle. Dark shadows snaked along the ground and in the trees. Faint noises creaked and groaned through the darkness. Ruth felt goosebumps pop up on her skin. Were those noises creatures on the prowl? Where were the people? And would they be able to help her?

"Hello?" Ruth called softly, not really sure of how loud she wanted to be. The endless trees seemed to swallow her words. "Umm..." Ruth continued, "is somebody out there?"

Suddenly, Ruth's eyes traced the outline of figures lurking behind the trees. Looking closer, she saw that their faces were painted, and they held assorted spears.

"Uh oh," Ruth breathed. "Do they think I'm a threat?" Her heart raced. "Umm, pardon me — "

The men jumped out, angrily pointing their spears at her and yelling in words Ruth couldn't understand.

"Ahh!" Ruth shrieked. "Don't hurt me! I'm not trying to threaten you!"

The tribesmen lunged forward, and Ruth had not a second to spare. Screaming, she stumbled through the jungle, limping across the soft, uneven ground.

.   .   .   .   .   .

Theodore stood in the crow's nest, keenly watching his surroundings, but he'd already looked as thoroughly as he could for any signs of Ruth. A gust of wind caught the mast, and Theodore nearly fell over. He grabbed for the rim of the crow's nest and straightened himself. As he glanced behind the ship, he suddenly remembered the island. His eyes widened, and he realized where Ruth might be trying to go.

"Charles!" he yelled. Charles was working in the rigging but glanced up when Theodore called his name. "Charles, tell the captain that Ruth might be on the island!"

"Oh!" Charles gasped. "I think you're right! Captain Edward!"

Captain Edward was on the forecastle. "What is it, Charles?" he called.

"Ruth's probably heading for the island! Remember? She was sweeping nearby when we were talking about it!"

Captain Edward's heart hammered as reality struck him. "I think you're right! She's in trouble! Augustus, hard over for the island! Sean! Apply fisherman's reef!"

Sean gasped. "But —"

"Do it!" Captain Edward commanded. "We might already be too late! Ruth doesn't know that tribe is dangerous!" A pained expression crossed his face.

.   .   .   .   .   .

Ruth hurried past rocks, trees, and bushes, not daring to look behind her. She tripped on her short leg and fell, but she forced herself back up. Her hear pounded, but she could see the beach now. "Oh, Lord, help!" she cried. "Help, God!"

Running through the sand was impossible, but Ruth limped as fast as she could for the shore. Sand kicked up behind as she sped for the water. Into her boat she flew and began rowing as fast as she possibly could. As she fumbled with the oars, Ruth glanced back at the island. The tribesmen were nowhere in sight. They must've decided a screaming girl didn't pose much of a threat. Ruth wished they had been people who could help her, because now she had nowhere to go but back out to sea.

She tried to row, but the waves rocked her boat and began spinning it around and around, faster and faster. Lighting flashed. Ruth was stranded in the stormy sea.

.   .   .   .   .   .

"Augustus!" Captain Edward exclaimed. "I told you hard over east."

"I did, sir," Augustus replied, his hands on the rudder, "but with the wind-over-tide like this, she won't answer."

"Ugh!" Captain Edward groaned again. "Is that all you've got? Try a different tack!"

.   .   .   .   .   .

Free

Tears stung in Ruth's eyes as the rain poured
down. Everything had gone so right. But now
everything was so wrong. Where could she go now?
"Should I try to go back to the ship?" she wondered
aloud. "No! That's not happening. I can't imagine what
they'd do to me now. A slave—a runaway, stowaway
slave. I tried so hard to treat them the way I should, but I
can't trust them to do the same for me!" Water trickled
from her eyes, joining the rain that splashed all over her
face. Lighting flashed through the foggy darkness.
Thunder crashed, as if taunting her loneliness. "They're
not safe. The island isn't safe. And out here isn't safe."
Ruth swallowed hard. "I'm stuck, God! Only You are
safe!"

A wave caught her boat and whipped it across
the ocean's surface. Ruth fell face-flat inside the tiny
vessel. Then, as she raised herself to her hands and
knees, she spotted a stream of water spewing in from
between two of the boards. Ruth hung her head. "God,
is this how this mess is going to end? Is it over?" she
wailed, trying to stop the leak with her hand. "Is
everything over?"

A huge shadow inched across Ruth's back, until
it completely engulfed her little boat. Ruth sniffled,
turned, and peered through the fog to see what could
make—

"Yes! It's her!" a voice shouted. A ship's edge
loomed over her. And it was the same ship she'd been
running away from!

"NO!" Ruth screamed. She vainly tried to row
away from the huge ship. *I'll be punished for running
away!* she thought. *How can this be happening?*

Sailors scrambled to the side of the ship where
Ruth was. Captain Edward tied a rope around his waist.
Sean tied the other end to the rail as Captain Edward
climbed over the edge of the ship.

Captain Edward began lowering himself down towards Ruth. Ruth panted as she frantically swung the oars around and around, putting every last ounce of her energy into escaping the men she'd been trying to get away from in the first place.

The sea was churning far too much for Ruth to get anywhere fast, and to make matters worse, the leak was making her boat tilt to one side. By the time Captain Edward had reached her, she was still within arm's reach of him.

Horrified, Ruth stood up and scrambled to the far end of her boat. She needed as much space from him as possible. Captain Edward's eyes widened. "Don't! You'll—"

Suddenly, the dinghy flipped, dumping Ruth into the water. Sharp pain shot up her foot and she felt a hard *thump* on her forehead. Everything went black.

Captain Edward gasped as the lifeboat hit Ruth in the head. She flopped into the water, and the lifeboat fell over her. Captain Edward, still tied to the rope, stepped onto the overturned dinghy and tried to reach underneath it to Ruth. He couldn't quite reach.

"I'm going to have to jump in!" he yelled to the other sailors. Captain Edward yanked the rope off his waist and splashed into the water.

It felt like forever before he could finally grab Ruth's arm. As he pulled her out, Captain Edward's stomach wrenched. Ruth's figure was motionless.

At last, he had her out of the water. He put Ruth on his shoulder and tied the rope back around his waist. He held onto Ruth with one hand and the rope with the other. "Pull us up!" he commanded the other sailors.

Alessio snatched the rope, and the rest of the men joined in. As he inched upward, Captain Edward glanced at Ruth. She was breathing, but her eyes were still closed.

"Hurry up, men!" Captain Edward commanded.

The men strained at the rope, and finally Captain Edward was close enough to hand Ruth to one of the sailors.

"Charles!" Captain Edward commanded. "Take her!"

Charles leaned over the rail, and Captain Edward shifted Ruth into his arms. He and the others glanced at Ruth, shocked to see she was unconscious. Charles held Ruth as Captain Edward climbed over the rail and onto the deck. After taking her back from Charles, Captain Edward sat Ruth up against the railing.

"Hector, you have medical training. Get over here and look at her," Captain Edward ordered.

Hector slid over beside Captain Edward. "She's breathing just fine," he said in his thick Spanish accent. "But she's got a nasty lump on her forehead. That probably accounts for why she is unconscious."

Captain Edward sighed, but then Ruth coughed. Her eyes slowly began to open.

"Mistress Ruth," began Captain Edward, trying to get her attention. But Ruth was still only half-awake.

After a few moments, Ruth's mind began to clear. Men were standing all around her. She felt the distinctive rocking motion of a ship. Suddenly she realized where she was, and she instinctively drew back. *No,* she thought. She was back on the ship with the cargo sailors.

Ruth's weary eyes glanced about her surroundings. Leonard's glare was just the same as before, and several of the other men looked angry too.

However, some of the sailors seemed worried. And then her eyes met Captain Edward's. His serious gray blue eyes seemed to say he was genuinely concerned about her. "Are you alright?" he asked.

Ruth gingerly touched the aching bump on her forehead. Her ankle surged with throbbing. Her heart raced with fear. "Not really," she answered, trying to keep her voice from trembling.

Captain Edward sighed, and Sean walked forward. "What did you think you were you doing?" he asked Ruth.

Ruth's heart thumped. "Don't ask!" she cried. "Just don't ask."

"We don't have to," Stephan said gruffly. "We all know what you were doing." He frowned at her.

Ruth swallowed hard, blinking back tears. She tried to straighten her confusion-riddled thoughts. Now what? Surely she couldn't trust these men to treat her properly. Or could she? Or did she just have to hope they would?

Captain Edward stared at her for several moments, as if he also didn't know how to respond. Once more, broken Ruth wondered if he cared enough to see the hurt that hid in her eyes. Ruth looked away from him. She didn't want him to see the tear that slipped down her cheek.

Captain Edward turned and stared at the ground for a few moments before turning to the other sailors. "From now on," he commanded, "I order that Mistress Brett's room is off-limits, and no one is to touch her, or you have me to deal with."

Alan quickly objected: "She doesn't *have* a room."

Free

Captain Edward looked at Ruth and thought a moment. Then he looked back up at the men. "You know that small room afore the main hold? That room will be hers. I want all of you to stay out of it. Do you understand?"

Stephan placed his hands on his hips. "What if we need to grab something out of it?"

Captain Edward's brow creased, and he hesitated. Then he said firmly, "You'll do it because I said so. If you go in there without telling me, you'll be in serious trouble."

Stephan walked away, and one by one the other sailors followed until only Captain Edward was left beside Ruth.

When Captain Edward finally began to walk away, Ruth was more than ready to get below deck and be alone. But as she stood up, the sharp pain that shot up her leg instantly reminded her that she had hurt her ankle. "Ouch!" she gasped, wincing as she fell over.

Captain Edward turned around. "Did you twist it?" he asked.

Ruth glanced up. She nodded in response to his question.

Captain Edward knelt down beside her. "May I look at it?" he asked, reaching toward her foot.

Ruth hesitated, but if he had just made rules to protect her, he wouldn't be trying to trick her and then hurt her. Ruth nodded again and pulled her foot to where he could examine it.

Captain Edward gently inspected her ankle. "It's twisted, but it doesn't look too bad." He glanced around for a piece of cloth. Not seeing any nearby, he unknotted his sash and pulled it off. Slowly, he began using it to skillfully wrap up the puffy ankle.

"Ah," said a taunting voice from behind. Captain Edward turned to see Alan, who continued, "And the captain just said no one was to touch her."

Captain Edward shook his head. Rather than fight a foolish argument, he said nothing. He continued wrapping Ruth's ankle and hoped Alan would go away.

But Alan persisted: "You know, if the captain isn't going to follow his own rules, we might as well make our own."

Captain Edward was thinking he might have to fight this argument after all, but just then Charles walked up and stood in front of Alan.

"Come now, chap," said Charles in an incredulous tone. "He said no one could touch her, meaning hurt her."

"No, all he said was that no one could touch her." Alan wasn't giving up.

"Give it up, Alan," Charles demanded. "He's the captain. He can do as he pleases. Besides, you know what he meant."

Alan turned away in a huff. Captain Edward sighed with relief, grateful Charles had taken care of it, and went back to wrapping Ruth's swollen ankle.

Ruth drew in a deep breath. She was still stressed about the situation, and watching Alan argue hadn't helped. But Ruth watched as Captain Edward finished wrapping her ankle in his sash.

Here was a sailor at least seeming like he cared about her. Captain Edward was much gentler than she had expected, and he was certainly gentler than the other men would probably be. And, too, he had just made rules to protect her. Perhaps now she would be safe until they reached land and she could *finally* go.

Free

Captain Edward tucked the loose end of the cloth into the wrapping. Gently setting her foot down, he looked up at Ruth.

A small smile crept onto Ruth's face. "Thank you," she whispered.

Captain Edward returned her smile. "My pleasure," he said with a nod. He rose to his feet and held out his hand to help Ruth up.

Ruth placed her hand in his and began trying painstakingly to pull herself up. Now that her good foot was injured, she was going to have to rest all her weight on her short leg. This was *not* going to be easy.

Ruth grimaced as her swollen ankle brushed the floor, but she lifted it up off the ground as at last she stood up.

She grabbed the railing as Captain Edward let go of her hand. "I know you're probably wanting to get some sleep, but since you were unconscious you need to stay up for a bit," he said. "Why don't you come sit over here by where I'll be working."

Ruth swallowed a whimper, but she obediently turned toward the direction Captain Edward was walking. Taking a hand off the rail, she began making one-foot hops toward a nearby barrel. She noticed that the wind had died down and that it wasn't raining anymore. But the deck was still slippery, adding to her difficulty.

It felt like forever, but Ruth reached the barrel. Ruth plopped down onto it and brushed a stray hair off her face. As she watched the sailors working, Ruth prayed silently. *Oh, God, is this my mission now — to treat these sailors as best as I can, despite their harshness? But I still don't have anywhere to truly* belong! *And when I was obedient, they didn't change a bit!* Ruth reached up to wipe her eyes before a tear could slip out.

Finally, a short while later, Captain Edward turned to Ruth and said, "Ruth, you can go to your room now."

Ruth didn't need to be offered twice. "Alright." She instantly grabbed the rail and pulled herself onto her good foot. "Where is it?"

"When you get down the hatch, it'll be the second to last door on the left."

"Alright. Thank you." Ruth hopped around the perimeter of the ship, holding onto the rail, until she was across from the stairs. She steadied herself, then let go of the rail and hopped toward the stairs as fast as she could. Arms flailing, she grabbed for the mast beside the hatch.

Looking down the stairwell, she remembered with dismay that there was no railing. So she lowered herself onto her short leg, holding out her injured foot. As she sat down, her sore ankle brushed the ground.

Grimacing, Ruth began sliding down each step individually. It probably looked silly to the sailors, but there wasn't anything *wrong* with it.

Eventually, Ruth reached the bottom of the stairs and stumbled as fast as she could for the end of the hall. She counted the doors twice to make sure she ended up in the right room. The last thing she wanted right now was to get in trouble for ending up in the wrong place.

As she opened the door, Ruth stared into the dirty, dusty, tiny room. It was hardly bigger than a closet, full of sacks and barrels and ropes. In the corner, there lay an old, small bed. Exhausted from her ordeal, Ruth shut the door and flopped onto the hard wooden cot. Ruth broke down and let herself cry. Tears trickled down her pale cheeks and onto the scratchy planks. Out above deck, the sun was rising; but Ruth felt as if she

Free

needed to sleep for a week! The weight of the world
around her settled heavily on her heart, but eventually,
Ruth drifted off.

Careena Campbell

Chapter Four

My Father's World

The heavens are telling of the glory of God; and their
expanse is declaring the work of His hands.

(Psalm 19:1 NASB)

*T*he door crashed open, and Ruth woke with a
start. First Mate Leonard stood in the doorway,
and he looked unhappy. Ruth bolted upright, expecting
him to shout at her again. To her surprise, he walked
away silently. Maybe because of the captain's orders.

Ruth sighed with relief and sat up on the edge of
the bed, yawning. She bumped her foot on the edge, and
the instant throbbing reminding her she needed to be
careful of her twisted ankle. But Ruth wasn't as upset
about it now. Her thoughts were so much clearer now
after her nap. She reached for the Bible and flipped it
open.

A few minutes later, Ruth began praying.
"Lord," she said, "I don't think I can hide my
discouragement anymore. I can't act 'perfect' any longer,
but maybe I was never supposed to. I can still honor
You, even in my imperfections."

Ruth thought of the story of Joseph in the
Bible—how he persevered a long, long time, and
eventually God rewarded him for his faithfulness.
Surely those years in prison must have been very hard.
But God was still looking out for Joseph, even in prison.
The Lord made the jailor trust Joseph and give him
responsibilities—a great privilege for a prisoner! Ruth

smiled. That had been her papa's favorite part of his favorite story.

A peaceful smile illuminated Ruth's face as she crawled out of bed. She leaned against the wall with her arm as she limped for the door, holding her wrapped ankle off the ground.

Just as Ruth grabbed the door handle, an object on the floor caught her eye. Whatever it was, it appeared to be shaped like a cross.

Ruth lowered to her hands and knees, being careful not to bump her ankle against the wall, and picked up the object. It was a small chunk of wood, no more than two inches long. The rugged, twisted bark resembled a cross.

Ruth grinned. She glanced around the room, looking for a string. Her eyes shifted to the hem of her dress. A stray thread hung off the edge. Ruth used her thumbnail to rip it off and poked the string into a slit in the wood.

The string wouldn't go through, but Ruth worked it and worked it, until, finally, a tiny end of thread poked through the other side of the wood. Ruth pinched it and pulled the string through.

"There," she said, holding it up. "Now it's a lovely necklace!" With a big smile, Ruth tied the string around her neck.

She fingered the cross shape and mused, "More than wearing a cross, I bear the name 'Christian'. Lord, please help me be a faithful representation of You."

Ruth hummed happily. Going up the stairs was difficult with her twisted ankle, but she managed. As she squinted in the bright mid-morning sunlight, she noticed the men were hard at work rowing.

"This is so unpleasant," grumbled Alessio.

Free

"Oy! It sure is," agreed First Mate Leonard grouchily. "You'd think with the wind we had this morning, there'd be more right now." Sweat ran down his forehead.

Ruth glanced over at Captain Edward. He was standing beside the mast, overseeing what the men were doing. She stood silently for a few moments. "Good morning, captain," she greeted rather tentatively.

"Good morning," Captain Edward returned.

"It's a beautiful day," Ruth remarked, soaking in the warm sunshine.

Captain Edward nodded. "It is."

Ruth paused for a moment. "Captain, what would you like me to do today?"

"Umm..." Captain Edward shifted uncomfortably. "Whatever. Just take it easier today."

Ruth felt grateful for his answer and turned to walk away.

"Oy!" yelled Hector, raising a hand. "Clean our cabin! It's filthy!"

Captain Edward glanced at Hector, then back at Ruth. "Please," he added for Hector.

Ruth hesitated momentarily, but then she nodded. "I'll see if I can," she agreed. Her parents had made a rule for her, to keep her safe: no going in men's bedrooms unless there was no one in it. And Ruth certainly still wanted to honor that rule.

So, Ruth limped back below deck.

"Oh, dear," she moaned, her face tightening. "I'm not sure I can manage this. This ankle hurts."

Ruth slowly made her way toward the sailor's quarters, delicately lifting her sore foot off the ground.

Ruth peered into the main bedroom. No one stood among the cots and trunks. *Oh, dear,* Ruth thought with a tinge of regret. *I guess I have to clean it, then.*

Ruth crawled over to her own room. Her eyes glanced up to the corner. The broom wasn't there. Ruth sighed and headed toward the galley. As she made the turn, her sore foot bumped the wall, instantly scolding her with throbbing. Ruth grimaced. This wasn't going well.

There it was, beside the table…on the floor. Good, now she wouldn't have to stand up to get it. Ruth grabbed the handle and turned until she was facing the door, still holding the broom beside her.

Little by little, Ruth carried the broom through the hall. From time to time she had to stop and regain her balance as the ship slowly rocked side to side, but she moved steadily forward until she was once again in the doorway of the sailors' room.

The room was still empty, so Ruth set to work. She sat on one of the beds as she swept the area around her. Indeed, Hector was right. It *was* filthy!

Ruth wasn't as discouraged as before, but thoughts of both contentment and confusion still tumbled through her mind.

Well, they're not being as rough with me now, Ruth thought. *Thank You, God.*

She bent over to reach the broom under the bed. "Am I going to be here *forever?*" she wondered. That thought was overwhelming, but Ruth tried to face it with truth. "Well, I can't change *forever;* God holds that. Lord, please help me stay positive."

As the broomstraws swished across the floor, Ruth tried to think of something to smile about. "Well," she mused, the corners of her mouth turning up, "I guess as a little girl, I always liked to pretend I was a cute little maid scrubbing floors with a kerchief over her hair. I guess now I'm not pretending the maid part anymore! But why did it seem like so much more fun back then?"

Ruth remembered a verse from Ecclesiastes 7:

"Say not thou, What is *the cause* that the former days were better than these? for thou dost not enquire wisely concerning this."

"Well, I guess that means I shouldn't look back and wish for the past just because it feels like it was better. Like how Philippians talks about 'forgetting those things which are behind, and reaching forth unto those things which are before.' God, I want to have Your peace and take this challenge one step at a time."

Thinking about her situation as a challenge gave Ruth extra motivation. Of course, it was not a challenge she had *wanted* to take on! But she tried to not let that prevent her from being confident that she could conquer this challenge with God's grace.

Just as Ruth swept the last dirt pile into an empty bucket she had found nearby, Captain Edward walked in. Ruth wobbled to her feet, turning to leave.

"Where are you going?" Captain Edward asked, watching her limp toward the door.

Ruth leaned against the wall as she quickly explained her parents' rule, then left the room with her awkward little steps. Captain Edward turned away silently, his gaze shifting to the thoroughly swept floor. Without realizing it, he smiled.

That night, Ruth crawled into bed with a tired but contented smile. The day had held its challenges, but God's grace had given her strength for each task as it had come. This time, the sheet on the old, creaky cot felt warm and comforting instead of scratchy and unwelcoming. As Ruth slept, she dreamed of being a kind maiden aboard a ship whose sailors would look out for her.

The next day passed much the same, and as evening fell, Ruth limped up to the top deck for some fresh air before bed. Unlike the nights before, the sailors were not making boisterous noise, so Ruth felt more comfortable being nearby.

She walked beside the mast, being careful of her sore ankle. It certainly wasn't as swollen as yesterday, and it no longer throbbed as badly if Ruth accidentally brushed it against the floor. But still, Ruth was cautious of putting any weight on it.

Several of the sailors were standing nearby, talking in serious tones. Ruth quickly realized something was wrong. She tried to make out what they were saying.

By his tone of voice, Captain Edward was evidently stressed. "Leonard, I told you it was a terrible idea for you to man the rudder!" he groaned. "Augustus knows these waters far better than you!"

"No kidding!" shouted Stephan. "A few miles off course could be the difference of death and survival out here!"

Ruth's eyes widened, but at the same time, an unexplainable peace flowed through her heart.

Stephan stepped away from the group and Ruth asked, "Sir, why wouldn't we survive?"

"Oh, there are all sorts of reasons," Stephan explained. "For one, we could run out of food and water. Then our crew could fall ill and leave us without enough manpower to make it back. The list goes on and on, really."

Free

Ruth nodded. "Of course." Still, this knowledge did not replace the peace in her heart with fear. God had supplied her soul with divine peace.

Stephan walked below deck. Captain Edward brought out his cross-staff. Augustus pulled out a compass, and the sailors began trying to find their bearings.

Ruth limped the few short steps to the edge of the ship. Her hands floated up to the railing as she gazed upwards. The night sky was encrusted with millions of brilliant stars, each twinkling one after the other. They stretched out all the way to the horizon, where they cast their reflections over the ocean. The sea, like a great blue blanket covered with shining sapphires, rocked back and forth as the wind gently caressed its water. The waves seemed to sigh in contentment, as if they were settling down to sleep, as they softly swooshed over each other.

Ruth's heart beat fast as she was overtaken with the beauty and the majesty of God's creation. She could not resist praising and thanking the Creator of this breathtaking scene, and her awe bubbled over in soft song.

"This is my Father's world,

and to my list'ning ears,

All nature sings and round me rings

The music of the spheres…"

The nearby sailors turned, surprised to hear the gentle strains of a song floating from the ship's edge.

"…This is my Father's world,

I rest me in the thought,

Of rocks and trees of skies and seas—

65

His hand the wonders wrought..."

For a moment, they watched the maiden fairly sing. Why was she so calm? Didn't she understand the danger they were facing?

But Ruth, for once, did not even notice them. She was swept up in the beauty of God's peace.

She reflected on her own situation as she sang the final verse:

"This is my Father's world;

O let me ne'er forget

That though the wrong seems oft so strong,

God is the ruler yet.

"This is my Father's world!

The battle is not done!

Jesus who died shall be satisfied,

And earth and heav'n be one.

"Yes," Ruth thought. "The battle is *not* done. God isn't finished with me, and He's not finished with the sailors, either. I will press on. I know He is still working!"

Ruth's heart swelled with joy and contentment. Leaning out over the ship's railing, she folded her hands to pray. "Lord," she whispered, "please bless the sailors and help them to come to know You. And help me to be brave even when things aren't this peaceful. Amen."

Ruth straightened up and smiled as she returned to her room for the night. Now she felt she could face her future, for God had reminded her of His presence.

Chapter Five

Rejoice, Ye Pure in Heart

Rejoice in the Lord always; again I will say, rejoice! Let your gentle spirit be known to all men. The Lord is near.

(Philippians 4:4,5 NASB)

A hh," Ruth sighed, wiggling her toes as she lay sprawled out in bed. Suddenly she sat up. If she was wiggling her toes, why wasn't her ankle hurting?

Having already finished her devotions, Ruth set the Bible aside and carefully turned to where her legs hung over the side of the bed. Gingerly, she brushed her toes on the floor. No pain. Very slowly, Ruth shifted a tiny bit of weight onto the foot. Her ankle ached a little in response, but it didn't throb. Ruth quickly shifted some more weight onto it.

Ouch. That hurt. Ruth drew her weight off the foot and stood up on the other one.

Well, Ruth thought as she hopped over to the door, *maybe now I can walk on it a little today!*

She made small one-foot hops until she reached the stairs, then decided to give her healing foot a try. Leaning on the wall for support, she placed her good foot on the first step, then lifted the other after it. Then she let her weight rest on her wrapped-up foot for a split second as she raised her good foot to the second step.

Well, it hurt a little bit, but it was worth not having to crawl up the steps. Ruth climbed the remaining stairs, each time going a little faster than the last.

At last she stood on the top deck. "Good morning, captain," she greeted cheerfully. She looked down at her dirty dress, then asked, "Sir, do you want me to wash some clothes?"

Captain Edward shrugged. "We'll do that when we get to shore."

"*If* we get to shore," piped up one of the men gloomily.

Ruth looked back up at Captain Edward and nodded, "Yes, sir," but her eyes widened. That meant she wouldn't get an opportunity to rinse off her dress either, and *that* meant she'd stay dirty and not smell good, either! *Oh, well,* Ruth thought. *I guess sailors don't really care about that. It's probably part of life on a ship.*

Captain Edward turned to Ruth, glancing down at her wrapped-up foot. "How's your ankle?" he asked.

Ruth nodded. "Much better, praise the Lord," she answered.

Captain Edward nodded. Ruth stood for a moment on the breezy deck, assessing in her mind what cleaning was left to be done. She'd wiped the table yesterday, and she'd already swept. Well, she could mop!

"Sir," Ruth asked, "if I don't use drinking water for cleaning, then what do I use?"

"Seawater." Captain Edward nodded toward the vast ocean. "Lower a bucket off the side of the ship and get some."

"Alright." Ruth made her way back to the galley to fetch a bucket. It was the same one she had used only three days earlier, when First Mate Leonard had knocked her to the ground. Ruth shook her head in an effort to forget the terrible moment and went searching for a rope.

First she checked the room she had been sleeping in. The tiny, filthy room was crammed with miscellaneous items. Even though the largest object in it was the bed, it was cramped. Ruth's eyes searched its perimeter for a rope, but her search proved unproductive. She considered checking the cargo hold, but how would she tell the difference between a rope the sailors owned and one they were merely transporting? Ruth decided to search the top deck.

Sure enough, beside the main mast sat a barrel, and on its lid lay a thick, coiled-up rope. Ruth limped over and picked it up. Glancing around, she decided she'd better ask permission before using it.

She limped over to a sailor who didn't appear to be doing anything. Captain Edward was nowhere in sight, otherwise she'd have asked him. "Pardon me, sir," she said timidly.

The sailor turned to face the short, teenage girl. "I'm Ronan."

"Alright, Master Ronan," Ruth nodded slowly. "May I use this rope?"

Ronan squinted, pulling back a hair that had blown into his face. "What for?"

"To get water. From the ocean, I mean. The captain said that's what to use…I mean since I'm cleaning and can't use drinking water." Ruth didn't sound like she knew what she was talking about, because, well, she really didn't.

"Whatever," Ronan shrugged. "Just don't lose it. And make *sure* the knot is tight," he added as if it were the most obvious thing in the world.

"I'll do my best," Ruth answered, limping back to where she had set the bucket. She sat down next to it and worked with the rope until she had tied a triple knot around the bucket's handle.

Ruth then limped over to the stern and placed the bucket to where it hung over the side of the ship.

Slowly, slowly, the bucket descended toward the ocean's surface. When at last it was lowered, the bucket simply floated atop the water.

"Well, that's not going to work," Ruth thought. "How do I tip it over so that it fills up?"

Ruth pulled the rope up a little, then swung it outward so the bucket landed farther out from the ship. This time, the bucket landed on its side, but only a small amount of water collected in it. Ruth gave little tugs on the rope until the bucket was halfway full.

Next Ruth began hoisting the bucket back up. She strained as she pulled hand-over-hand on the rope. The bucket was only halfway full, but it was still heavy and difficult to pull up—especially with the poor leverage her legs provided. She noticed that Captain Edward was watching nearby.

Suddenly, Ruth was dismayed to see the knots were beginning to give way. The first one slipped off, and the second quickly followed. "Oh, come on!" Ruth breathed. Her heart hammered to think of the sailors' reaction if she lost their bucket. Desperately she began flailing with the rope as quickly as she possibly could.

The final knot began slipping, and Ruth knew what was going to happen. So did Captain Edward, who jumped over and grabbed the rope from her. But it was too late. The rope spun off the bucket's handle, and the bucket fell into the ocean.

Free

Captain Edward looked at Ruth disapprovingly. Ruth felt her face turn red, and a lump caught in her throat. "Sorry," she gulped. Her face grew redder when she realized several other sailors were watching. "I tied the knots as tightly as I could!" she protested.

"It's just a bucket," Stephan shrugged calmly. Then he walked away, uninterested.

Ruth was surprised he wasn't upset with her, but this time it looked like Captain Edward was. She braced herself for a harsh rebuke as he closed his eyes and took a deep breath. She wondered if he was thinking that it had been a terrible idea to keep her on the ship; that she didn't know how to do anything. Ruth sighed. She hoped this situation wasn't going to change the captain's usually kind attitude toward her.

When Captain Edward walked away without a word, Ruth felt relieved. She turned to go below deck and limped straight past the galley. The mopping could wait.

Later, as Captain Edward walked through the corridor, he marveled at the clean, recently swept floors and smiled. The incident with the bucket had done nothing to change his fondness of the maiden who had cleaned them.

Ruth limped by, once again humming a cheery tune. Captain Edward stopped her. "Ruth."

Ruth stopped. Quietly she waited for him to continue. But it seemed he wasn't quite sure what he wanted to say.

Slowly, Captain Edward began. "You're not strong," he said in a subdued voice. "You're just a girl."

Ruth looked at him a bit more closely, surprised by this strange beginning. What was he trying to say?

Captain Edward continued: "And yet, you never snapped back at Leonard or resented my authority, even though we really have no right to make you work for us. It seems," he said thoughtfully, looking down at the floor, "that you possess a strength none of us have." His gray eyes looked deep into her face. "Is it because of your faith in God?"

Ruth's eyes widened, and her face lit up in a glorious smile. *Oh, Lord!* she thought. *You're seriously giving me this opportunity!* Ruth opened her mouth, but quietly paused to ask for God's wisdom. *Help me say just what You want,* she prayed silently.

Ruth's face glowed with Jesus' passion and love as she proclaimed, "YES!

"God certainly gives me strength. I mean, not that I've felt great at every moment." Ruth paused before continuing, thinking about all the hardships she'd been facing. "You yourself have seen my discouragement. But remembering Scripture verses and stories and the times God has been faithful helps me. It seems in my experience," she added as God handed her more words to say, "that courage comes from focusing on who God is and not on your situation!"

Captain Edward nodded, pondering her words. "You've been showing us all something about what Christian service looks like, even though you're just a girl — and a servant against your own will." He didn't realize he was giving Ruth a great compliment.

Ruth smiled wider. "I'm free in Jesus!" Ruth realized that truth was something she herself had been needing to remember.

Captain Edward stared at the floor. "My parents were Christians."

Ruth nodded, but felt her heart skip a beat. "Mine too."

72

Free

Captain Edward looked back up and nodded. "Thank you, Ruth."

"It was my pleasure!" Ruth declared joyfully. As she turned away, encouragement filled her heart and flooded through all her veins. As she walked back to the galley, she burst into victorious song: "Rejoice, ye pure in heart! Rejoice, give thanks and sing!" The joy of shining for Christ had filled her with energy to live joyfully for the rest of the day.

Careena Campbell

Chapter Six

Stand Up, Stand Up for Jesus

Who are you to judge the servant of another? To his own master he stands or falls; and he will stand, for the Lord is able to make him stand.

(Romans 14:4 NASB)

woosh…swish…swoosh…slosh. One of Augustus' eyes popped open. Where was the *slosh* coming from? Quietly, he slipped out of bed to figure out its source.

SPLASH! His feet landed on water. "Oy, NO!" he shouted. He quickly jumped from the room and pounded on the door of Captain Edward's cabin. "Captain! Wake up! We've taken on water!"

"What!" Captain Edward half-yelled, throwing himself out of bed. Appearing at the door, his eyes locked on the standing water at the end of the hall. "Alas! You're right! Men, men, get up! All hands on deck!"

Sailors began scrambling out of bed and into the hall. Captain Edward was already giving orders: "You three, find the leak! GO! Everyone else, we need to bail this water out of here!"

In the room down the hall, Ruth awoke to chaotic noises piercing midnight silence. The sailors were making a lot of noise just outside her room. What were they doing now?

Ruth cautiously slipped out of bed and peeked out her door. Sailors scrambled up and down the hall with buckets. Down the hall, water flooded the floor.

"What's going on?" Ruth mumbled sleepily.

"There's a leak somewhere!" Charles shouted.

"It's in the cargo hold!" declared Alessio.

Ruth gasped. "Does that mean we're *sinking?*"

"It might," replied another sailor seriously.

Ruth looked at all the water just standing there. "What can I do?"

"Help us!" answered Alan, hauling a heavy bucket up the stairs.

Ruth thought a moment. She could picture herself losing her footing in all that water. And with her ankle…well, most of the time it didn't bother her anymore, but she still had to be careful. Well, she would try it. They needed everyone's help. She raced to the galley and snatched a small bucket. Splashing back into the hall, she filled it up and walked toward the stairs.

Walking slowly to keep her balance, Ruth carried the pail up each step. Once she reached the top deck, she limped swiftly over to the ship's edge and dumped the bucket's contents into the ocean. As she hurried back to the stairs, sailors brushed by her.

"I have the chalk and hammer!" shouted Hector.

"Aye!" yelled someone else, and they raced below deck.

As Ruth wobbled up with another pail full of water, she tried to see if the boat was tilting any. She couldn't tell, but she wondered what they'd do if it did start sinking.

Ruth felt a wave of tiredness sweep over her as she walked back down, but it was obvious no one would be returning to bed anytime soon.

The sailors rushed around, trying to remove the water as quickly as possible. From what she observed, Ruth assumed the leak had been repaired. There was less standing water, and the sailors seemed not quite so panicked. She continued trying to help as much as she could, but inwardly Ruth wondered if she was just in the way. Various thuds and splashes pierced the midnight silence as the sailors scrambled about.

Captain Edward's voice called out: "Hector! What's our status?"

Hector appeared at the door of the cargo hold, holding a hammer. He was breathing hard and sweat trickled down his face. "It's fixed. We're safe."

Captain Edward sighed with relief, and Ruth exclaimed, "Praise the Lord!"

Several of the sailors stared at her, but Ruth didn't care. God's hope shone through her smile.

Forty minutes later, most of the water had been removed from below deck, and Ruth decided to take a break. Standing on the top deck, she noticed Captain Edward, First Mate Leonard, and several others standing in a group nearby.

Ruth wondered when she could go back to bed, but she didn't figure it was worth interrupting to ask. Going to bed was an item of least importance right now! As she breathed in the cool ocean air, she could hear the men talking nearby:

"Well, this is even more serious now," said Charles.

"I know," Captain Edward agreed. "The ship has been compromised, and we still aren't quite certain where we are."

"I believe we're in the southern end of the Bay of Biscay," First Mate Leonard suggested.

"No, we went by that island, so we're in the *northern* end of it," objected Augustus.

"Yes, but then we drifted…"

As the sailors argued over their location, Ruth was once more enamored by the stars. She knew the situation was serious, but God had placed a covering of peace over her heart.

"'Rejoice, give thanks and sing,'" she whispered to herself. "Jesus, please help me rejoice. And help the sailors become Christians. Amen."

Ruth reached down to squeeze water out of the hem of her skirt. Glancing around, she decided she could go to bed now. The sailors appeared to be finished hauling water, and even though she was still a little wet, she wanted to get to sleep. Her heart was still trying to slow down its racing from the midnight excitement, but as she lay in bed, God's peace brought sweet rest to her soul.

The next morning, Ruth yawned as she walked slowly up the stairs. As she glanced around, it seemed everyone else was particularly tired too—especially Augustus, who was leaning against one of the mast poles.

As Ruth stood on the sunny deck, trying to wake up, she saw several sailors talking nearby. She wasn't close enough to understand what they were saying, but she assumed they were discussing the dangers they were facing. Their composed but serious voices reminded Ruth of her own dear father.

Free

Ruth turned away from the men and looked out over the endless ocean. Her thoughts shifted to a problem that was at hand.

It's Sunday, she thought, *which means I shouldn't do any cleaning, because it's the day of rest. They may be angry about that. But it's the right thing to do,* she decided calmly and confidently.

Nearby, the sailors had ended their conversation and were going their separate ways. Augustus walked over to Ruth and said, "Mistress, when you make the midday meal today, make half of what you normally would."

Ruth looked confused. Without realizing it, she asked, "Why?"

"We need to conserve our food supply," Augustus explained. "We don't want to run out of food before finding land."

Ruth nodded. "Yes, sir. I will do that."

Augustus walked away, rather slowly, to continue with his morning duties.

Ruth stood quietly for a few moments. "Well," she decided, "since it's Sunday, it'd be a fine idea to spend some extra time studying God's Word." She turned to walk to her room, but First Mate Leonard stopped her.

"Oy. You," he began, "I want you to clean the rails today. I'm tired of my hands always being filthy from touching them."

Ruth took a deep breath. *Did it have to be him?* she thought. *I'm sorry, God. That was not the right response. I should be happy to have a chance to "give an answer" to him about "the hope within me."* Ruth paused for a moment, considering her response. Then she spoke, her words filled with God-inspired confidence in what she believed.

"I beg your pardon, sir," she began respectfully, "but I need to not do any cleaning today. It's—"

"Why?" First Mate Leonard interrupted. His sharp, stern face turned toward her.

"Because it's Sunday," Ruth answered, "which is the day of rest. God commanded His people to honor the Sabbath day. I need to obey Him and rest today. But I'd be happy to do it tomorrow." Ruth waited for a response. Her heart hammered, but knowing she was standing up for what God had told her gave her courage unlike any other.

First Mate Leonard put his hands on his hips and stared at her fiercely. Finally, he said, "Fine." Away he walked, without another word.

Ruth sighed with relief and felt happiness once again flooding her heart. She had stood up for what's right, and God had protected her from Leonard. With a joyful skip in her step, she hopped back to her room, the hem of her dress bouncing along with her.

She half-leaped onto her cot, which squeaked loudly in protest. Bending down, she picked up the Bible off the floor and flipped to Jeremiah. As a little girl, she'd always enjoyed reading the thrilling stories of Jeremiah, and it had been awhile since she'd read them.

But as she flipped through the book, looking for a place to read, chapter 29 caught her eye. Quickly, she realized why God had brought her there.

Her eyes skimmed verse 7:

"And seek the peace of the city whither I have caused you to be carried away captives, and pray unto the Lord for it: for in the peace thereof shall ye have peace."

Ruth closed her eyes as she thought about the wonderful verse. "Well, my welfare is bound up in the ship's welfare," she mused. "If it were to sink, it would be just as bad for me as for the other sailors!

"As for the praying part," she continued, "I've been doing that already! How encouraging that I was praying for the sailors, even though they've been harsh to me, and God guided me to a verse that told me that's exactly what He wanted me to do!"

Ruth grinned and set aside "her" Bible. "I'll pray some more right now.

"Dear Heavenly Father, I thank You for these verses. Thank You for encouraging me. Please help me to continue to find peace in knowing this is the mission You have given me, and joy when I've been faithful to complete that mission. In Jesus' Name, amen."

Ruth's eyes opened and landed on another verse—verse 11. It was a verse she had heard many times before, but never before had it meant so much to her.

"For I know the thoughts that I think toward you, saith the LORD, thoughts of peace, and not of evil, to give you an unexpected end."

"'An unexpected end,'" Ruth whispered. "God is planning my future, so I needn't worry about it. Who knows? Maybe He has some surprises in store for me. After all, He *is* my hope—and my future.

"I guess…" Ruth sighed, but continued to feel hope shining in her heart. "I guess if this is where You have placed me, it's where I belong. And I am not alone, because You are with me!"

Ruth flipped to Ephesians 6, the passage she had read the first day she was captive.

"Servants, be obedient to them that are *your* masters according to the flesh, with fear and trembling, in singleness of your heart, as unto Christ; Not with eyeservice, as men-pleasers; but as servants of Christ, doing the will of God from the heart; With good will doing service, as to the Lord, and not to men: Knowing that whatsoever good thing any man doeth, the same shall he receive of the Lord, whether *he be* bond or free."

"God," Ruth whispered, "in light of this verse, I want to somehow go beyond what they ask of me. Give me joy because I am 'doing the will of God from the heart.' Thank You for the great moments You've already—"

Ruth's quiet thoughts were interrupted by a knock at the door. Energetically, she hopped up and opened the door. There stood Captain Edward.

"Yes?" Ruth greeted with a joyful smile.

Captain Edward sighed before responding. "Are you going to make us dinner soon?"

Ruth thought a moment. *Well, she thought, it's a bit earlier than when I normally make it. But I certainly can.*

"Certainly," she agreed.

Ruth walked out from her room across the hall to the galley. She began pulling out ingredients, placing them in the pot over the fire. It was almost like a routine, she'd done it so many times before.

Ruth had her back turned to him, and when she turned, she saw Captain Edward in the doorway, leaning on the doorjamb. He was deep in thought, eyebrows furrowed, stroking his beard. Ruth observed his expression. It was as if he was upset, worried, or stressed about something.

"Is something wrong?" Ruth asked.

Free

Captain Edward glanced up at her but did not respond. Ruth turned back to her work.

"Mistress Ruth," he said finally. Ruth turned around. Captain Edward paused to compose himself.

"When you were talking to Leonard just now," he began, motioning behind him, "you spoke up and told him you weren't going to do what he asked because it was against what you believed. You weren't nervous or anything, you just said what you were going to do and why."

Ruth chuckled. "Well, if I'm being honest, I *was* nervous!"

"But you didn't let that stop you from standing up for what you believe in. Even though you didn't know if Leonard might try to hurt you for disobeying him," Captain Edward added seriously.

Ruth nodded. "You're right. He might have. But I'm going to do what God says, no questions asked. Even if I got killed for it, I'd still obey Him. People can hurt me or even take my life from me, but they can't take Jesus from my side. The Bible says, 'neither death, nor life…shall be able to separate me from the love of God.' I'd rather lose my life telling someone about Jesus than live and ignore an opportunity to tell them something that could save them from hell." Ruth's face glowed with the joy that comes from telling others about Jesus.

Captain Edward raised his eyebrows and nodded. "Alright. Thank you." He then turned and disappeared into the hallway.

Ruth hummed a happy tune as she fiddled with the food. In her mind, she made up her own song:

"For now this is where I belong,

Shining for God; my life like a song.

It may be hard and it may be rough,

But holding to Him is surely enough."

Her heart was still humming hours later when she skipped up the stairs, Bible in hand. The stars winked from high above, reminding her that God had brought her safely through another day. Ruth's eyes were practically glued to the shimmering sky as she limped to the edge of the ship. She sat down on a barrel, her gaze turned to the overhead canopy of glitter.

Ruth opened her Bible and began reading by the light of the full moon and a nearby lantern. The last verse she read before closing the pages was Galatians 6:9. "And let us not be weary in well doing: for in due season we shall reap, if we faint not."

Ruth yawned as she set the Bible on the floor. With a happy sigh, she folded her arms onto the railing and rested her chin on them. The cool evening breeze danced with stray wisps of her hair. Her eyelids drooped as she gazed over the shimmering ocean. Her mind wandered sleepily, and soon Ruth's eyes closed.

Captain Edward had just finished overseeing the securing of the ship for the night. Satisfied the men were properly completing their duties, he began walking to the hatch to return to his cabin for the night. On his way, he caught a glance of a figure resting against the ship's railing.

He walked over to Ruth. He smiled as he realized she had fallen asleep! Chuckling softly, he looked out over the vast ocean. A brisk breeze blew across the deck, and even though it was barely a flinch, Captain Edward noticed the sleeping girl shiver. A thought crossed his mind, and smiled as he stroked his beard. He glanced around, making sure none of the men were watching to tease him. Then, he turned back to Ruth. Smiling, he slipped off his coat and gently laid it across her shoulders. After he was satisfied the coat was tucked securely around her, he straightened up and walked below deck.

"It's the least I can do," he thought fondly.

Careena Campbell

Chapter Seven

Cared For

Since we have gifts that differ according to the grace
given to each of us, *each of us is to exercise them
accordingly:* …if service, in his serving; or he who
teaches, in his teaching; or he who exhorts, in his
exhortation; he who gives, with liberality; he who leads,
with diligence; he who shows mercy, with cheerfulness.

(Romans 12:6-8 NASB)

*T*he sun's spreading rays warmed the air
invitingly, beckoning those still asleep to arise
and embrace a new day. Captain Edward walked up to
the top deck and was met with the cheery warmth. He
nodded a hello as the night watchman climbed down
from the ladder. Walking out further onto the deck,
Captain Edward noticed the four men whose job it was
to lift the anchor. Their faces were turned toward Ruth
as one mumbled to the others. Ruth was in their way.

Hector stepped toward Ruth, but Captain
Edward waved him off. "I'll wake her up."

Hector walked back toward the group, and
Captain Edward stood next to Ruth. She was still sound
asleep, in just the same position as the night before.
Captain Edward called her name. "Ruth."

Ruth awoke with a start. Her sleepy eyes
squinted in the bright morning sunlight, as if surprised
it were already morning. She looked over at Captain
Edward, then glanced down at the coat draped over her.
Instantly, Ruth knew whose it was. Shyly, she
straightened up and pulled the coat off. As she stood up,

she held it out to Captain Edward. "Thank you," she whispered.

Captain Edward grinned. "It was my pleasure." He draped the coat over his arm and turned to walk away. Ruth bent over and picked up the Bible.

Captain Edward turned back to her and stopped. "May I have that?"

Ruth obediently handed him the Bible.

Taking it, Captain Edward thumbed through the old, yellowed pages. "I didn't know I still had this." At that, he walked away to continue with his day.

Ruth, now without a Bible, wasn't sure what to do. But she was glad Captain Edward had his Bible! Maybe now he would even start reading it!

Ruth wondered if it was time to ask First Mate Leonard for her Bible again. She walked around on the deck, hoping to spot him.

As she looked around, she noticed Augustus walking up the stairs. But once he reached the top deck, he just stopped and slumped his shoulder against the mast. He stared at the floor and ran his hand through his bedraggled brown hair, looking exhausted.

Captain Edward eyed him. "If you need to rest, you have my permission," he told Augustus.

Augustus sighed and just stood there for several moments before walking back down the stairs. Ruth watched him closely as he slowly shuffled down the steps.

Is he ill? Ruth thought. *If he is, I want to help him. But what rugged sailor is going to want a silly young girl to take care of him?*

Still, Ruth wanted to help Augustus, so she slipped down the stairs into the hallway. Only a few steps away, Augustus sat on a barrel. He was leaning forward, holding his head in his hands. Quietly Ruth stepped over to him. She tried to think of something to say. It felt awkward to just stand silently next to him.

Ruth could only seem to draw a blank. "Umm…"

Augustus turned to look at her.

"Um —" Ruth hesitated. "Um, are you feeling alright?"

Augustus stared at her blankly.

"Um, if you come into the galley, I can help you," Ruth added awkwardly.

Augustus puckered his brow as if her offer seemed strange. Ruth, who honestly hadn't expected a great response, moved on to the galley to decide what to do for the day. While she considered her options, she grabbed a rag and began scrubbing on the table.

"Well, I told First Mate Leonard I would clean the rails today, so I need to do that. I also never mopped. So —"

Ruth looked up to see Augustus walking in. She watched as he shuffled to the back of the room and sank into a chair. He leaned back and rested his head against the wall. His face was flushed, Ruth noticed.

Ruth set down her rag and limped over to him. She hesitantly held out her hand, as if to feel his forehead. Augustus shrugged, so she placed her hand to his brow. *Yes,* she thought, nodding to herself. *He's got a fever.*

Ruth looked down into his weary eyes. "I'll be right back," she promised.

Ruth hurried down the hall and scaled the stairs to the top deck. She grabbed a nearby small bucket and ran across the deck, pulling a coiled-up rope off the top of a barrel that was sitting beside the mast.

She fumbled with the rope and bucket as she came to the edge of the ship. Working quickly, she looped and threaded and pulled and tightened the rope until there were seven knots around the bucket's handle. Yes, she was sure there were seven. Surely now the bucket wouldn't fall.

Swiftly Ruth lowered the bucket toward the water's surface. She made sure to fill it less full than last time. After hauling it back up, she took it and hurried back down the stairs. Her ankle didn't bother her at all anymore.

Sailors noticed her stumbling around. Ruth didn't care if she looked odd. She was on a mission. As she neared the galley, she slowed her pace, stepping quietly into the small room.

Placing the bucket on the floor, Ruth knelt next to Augustus. She glanced around for a piece of fabric to use. There was none in the room, except for her rag, which was already a little dirty. She would have used her sash, but then her wrap-around dress wouldn't stay together. The rag would have to do. She snatched it off the table and dipped it into the cold water. Augustus heaved a sigh and shivered as Ruth placed the damp cloth to his forehead.

Footsteps creaked in the hall, and First Mate Leonard appeared at the doorway. His hair was particularly bedraggled, and there were dark circles under his eyes. In a scratchy voice he asked, "How much drinking water do we have left?"

"I'm not sure," Ruth responded. "Do you want me to check?"

Leonard shrugged.

"I was already going to go get some," Ruth insisted.

First Mate Leonard looked at her. "Fine, then."

Ruth grabbed a mug and stood up. As she walked out the doorway, she noticed how weary First Mate Leonard seemed. With caring eyes, she observed the slumped way he was standing. "Sir," she asked bravely, "Are you alright?"

Instantly, First Mate Leonard straightened up. "I'm fine," he sternly snapped. With that, he walked back down the hall and up to the top deck.

Ruth sighed, and turned to walk to the cargo hold. She could feel the ship rocking, just like it always did. She still wobbled a bit as it rocked, but not nearly as much as she used to. As she walked, she prayed quietly. "God, I'm not sure what's going on with the sailors. Augustus has fallen ill, and now it looks like First Mate Leonard might be ill too. Give me strength to do what I need to do no matter what happens."

She came to the galley and located the water barrels. Taking note of the water level in each one, she filled the mug and walked out. She came to the top deck and found First Mate Leonard. "There are four full ones left, and one that's about one-fourth full," she said.

Leonard nodded and turned back to Stephan and Hector. Ruth walked back down the steps and into the galley. She sat down next to Augustus a gently handed him the cup.

Augustus slowly took a sip. As he handed the cup back to Ruth, Ruth heard someone coming down the stairs. In the doorway appeared a blond young man whom Ruth hadn't seen much before.

"What are you doing, Augustus?" he asked, leaning his hands on the doorjamb.

Ruth spoke for Augustus. "He's not feeling well, so he's taking a break."

"Oh," replied the sailor, fidgeting with his tangled blond hair. He stood silently in the doorway for several moments, staring at the floor.

"What's your name, sir?" Ruth asked.

The man looked up at her. "Jonas," he responded.

"Alright, Jonas," Ruth said cheerfully. "What are you up to today?"

Ruth waited for an answer, but Jonas only shrugged. Ruth noticed how he sighed, swallowed hard, and blinked his tired eyes. *Hmm,* Ruth thought. *He sure looks like he's not feeling well either.* Ruth stood up and walked over to where Jonas was standing. "Are you feeling alright?"

Jonas glanced at her with tired eyes, then shrugged and folded his arms across his chest. Ruth reached up as if to feel his forehead. It was her way of silently asking if he would mind. Jonas squinted at her. "What are you doing?"

Ruth drew her hand back. "I just wanted to see if you have a fever."

"I don't."

Ruth almost smiled. The truth was, she already knew he had a fever. She could tell just by looking at him. His face was that flushed shade that Ruth's mother had taught her was the tell-tale sign.

Ruth looked at Jonas. "Well, you can think what you'd like, but I'm pretty sure you've got one," she said with an understanding smile. Then, in response to the shocked look on Jonas's face she shook her head and said, "There's no shame in that. I've had one before; it's no fun." Ruth found herself surprised at her own boldness. "Come on," she said, nodding her head toward where Augustus was sitting "Come sit down and rest a bit. I won't mind."

Jonas looked at Ruth, then at Augustus, then back down at Ruth. He then followed her silently to the back of the room and lowered into one of the other chairs. Ruth offered him the mug of water.

As Jonas took a sip, Captain Edward called from the hallway: "Jonas! Jonas, where'd you —" Captain Edward paused as he glanced into the galley. Ruth was standing beside Augustus and Jonas, who were sitting down and looked poorly. "Do I need to call Hector?" he asked Ruth.

Ruth glanced over at Augustus. "Well…I think that would be a good idea," she answered.

Captain Edward's brow creased. "Alright, I'll go find him." Captain Edward turned to leave.

"Oh! Captain, wait!" Ruth cried, springing up after him.

Captain Edward stopped, so Ruth began, "Sir, I think they need to be in their own beds. But I can't go in their rooms, you know. So, um…would you mind asking some of the men to move their beds into the mess room?"

Captain Edward chuckled. "You just never give up, do you?"

Ruth grinned, but felt that she should respond in case it wasn't supposed to be a compliment. "Is that a bad thing?"

Captain Edward shook his head. "No, no. It's good. Of course I'll ask the men to do that."

"Thank you," Ruth said with a nod, and she walked back to the galley.

Captain Edward climbed the stairs up to the top deck and walked toward Sean. "Hey," he said. "I need you to move Jonas's and Augustus's beds into the mess room."

"Why?" Sean questioned.

"They're ill," Captain Edward explained, "and Ruth is taking care of them."

"Why can't they just be in the bedroom?" Sean objected.

"That wouldn't be...appropriate," Captain Edward answered.

Sean shrugged. "Sure, I guess." He started toward the stairs. "I'll tell Hector about this, too."

"Thank you," Captain Edward answered. He then turned to Alan, who was standing nearby. "Help him, would you?"

Alan narrowed his eyes. "There's nothing wrong with them staying in the cabin. I'm busy doing other things," he said, and then walked away.

Captain Edward sighed. He then turned to Stephan and motioned for him to join Sean.

Stephan walked down the stairwell to find Sean painstakingly dragging Augustus's cot into the hall. "They're a bit of a challenge to get out of the doorway," Sean said without looking up. He shoved the squeaky cot toward the opposite wall. "I had to turn mine a bit."

Stephan stepped into the bedroom and began scooting Jonas' bed toward the door. Sean picked up Augustus' cot and carried it through the door of the mess room. When he came out, Sean leaned against the wall and absentmindedly tapped his fingers against it.

He drew in a deep breath, his eyes slowly turning upward.

At that moment, Ruth stepped out of the galley. She opened her mouth to speak, but then she saw Sean leaning against the wall, staring up at the ceiling. That in itself wasn't worth noting, except that his deep brown African face seemed flushed.

Ruth, who was becoming rather good at noticing when someone was feeling ill, silently watched him for a moment. Then she asked, "Master Sean, are you alright?"

Sean turned toward her and frowned. "I'm fine," he told her firmly.

Ruth hesitated. She couldn't help but wonder if he was feeling worse than he wanted to show. But she knew it wasn't her business to figure out. She turned to leave, but Hector called her: "*Señorita.*"

Ruth turned, and for a moment was surprised he was addressing her by a Spanish title. But then she remembered Hector was Spanish. Knowing some Spanish herself, she answered him in Spanish. "*Sí, Señor?*"

Hector looked surprised. "You speak Spanish?"

Ruth shrugged. "A little," she answered.

Hector nodded, looking down at the little book he was holding. In Spanish, he asked Ruth how many of the men were sick.

Ruth thought a moment. "Augustus, Jonas...well, Leonard..."

Hector nodded understandingly, writing in his little book. "*Gracias.*"

Sean looked at Ruth in surprise. "Where'd you learn Spanish?"

95

"Well, I've lived in Spain for…" Ruth paused, and for a moment a hurt look crossed her face. "…For two years."

Sean nodded. He hadn't seen the look because Ruth had already replaced it with another smile. She stepped over to Hector and peered over his arm at the book. On the page, there were two columns — one in English and one in Spanish. At the top of the English column was the title "Binnacle List." Ruth assumed that was the name for a list of sick sailors. Hector finished writing by signing his name next to the day's date.

"You have very nice handwriting," Ruth complimented.

Hector looked at her, and so did Sean and Stephan. Ruth laughed nervously, realizing they thought whatever she had just done was weird. "What?" Ruth laughed. "I'm just being encouraging, just like God does for me!" She walked down the hall with a skip in her step. "Thanks for moving the beds!"

The men stood quietly for a moment. Once he felt certain Ruth was out of earshot, Sean turned to Stephan and Hector. "What is wrong with her?"

Hector cocked his head. "One would begin to wonder if she's after romance."

Stephan snorted at the idea. "Well, she's not going to find it here."

"I doubt that's what she's after," Sean added. "It'd be different if she treated only one of us that way, but she's that way to all of us." Lowering his voice, he added, "Even Leonard."

Hector shrugged. "I suppose you have a point."

"But still," Sean continued skeptically. "Why is she so happy like that? She's a captive girl — a slave at that! — on a ship full of men who don't really care about her. And yet, she's always smiling, singing, and offering to help us in whatever way she can. How can she be like that all the time?"

"I don't know, but I know one thing that's *not* making me happy," Alan said sourly, walking up from the other end of the hall. "You making all this unnecessary racket over some servant girl when I've got a headache!"

Stephan huffed. "Well, maybe you should at least *tell* us to be quiet before getting mad about it!"

Just then, Ruth came back down the hall. She heard their angry voices, and her eyes looked concerned. She cocked her head at the men, wondering what was going on. The look on her face told them she was worried someone else was sick.

Stephan sighed disapprovingly, Sean shook his head, and Alan frowned at Ruth. "I'm fine," he said sternly.

Ruth looked a little hurt. Why were they upset when she just wanted to help people? *I guess Mother said men don't like anyone to act like there's something wrong with them,* Ruth thought. *But all I want is just to help.*

Ruth felt her heart sink a little, but she smiled anyway. "Alright, Alan," she agreed. "I just wanted to make sure you were alright." Ruth made her way to each of the two cots that now sat in the mess room, fluffing each pillow and turning down the covers until they were smooth and crisp. She tried to ignore the fact that the blankets were filthy. She then stepped over to the galley, where Augustus and Jonas sat, their flushed faces waiting for her.

"We've got your beds ready," she said gently.

Augustus nodded, and with a sigh, pulled himself to his feet. His arm swung out, reaching for the wall, and he scrunched his eyes shut.

Ruth's brow furrowed. "Are you dizzy?"

Augustus nodded, his breathing heavy.

Ruth thought a moment. "Why don't you sit down again, and I'll be right back."

Augustus sank back onto the chair, and Ruth walked back to the hall. "Master Sean, I —"

That's when Ruth saw Sean sitting on a barrel, his eyes closed, snoring. Ruth smiled — he'd decided to rest after all — but then her eyebrows furrowed. Turning to Stephan, she asked, "Is Sean usually a pretty deep sleeper?"

Stephan snickered. "You better believe he is. Slept right through the alarm bell once."

"Alright." Ruth carefully and quietly reached out her hand and felt Sean's forehead. Ruth sighed. She turned to Stephan, her eyes silently telling him Sean, too, had a fever. Ruth pointed questioningly to the cabin.

Stephan nodded. He knew what she was asking. He went to drag Sean's bed into the mess room.

Just then, Captain Edward walked down the stairs.

"Oh!" Ruth exclaimed, though her voice a whisper. "Captain, I was just going to look for you. Augustus is really dizzy. I was wondering if, well, you could make sure he stays steady as he walks to his bed."

A concerned look shadowed Captain Edward's face, and for a moment he didn't respond.

"Is that an improper thing to ask?" Ruth suddenly wondered if her boldness had gone too far.

"No, no," Captain Edward answered, his gaze still far away. "It's perfectly fine. I'm just wondering if there's something more we should be doing."

Ruth smiled. "Pray."

Captain Edward sighed, his gaze shifting to the floor. "Pray," he mumbled. But he said no more. Instead, he walked into the galley to help Augustus.

He walked through the door and found Augustus with his head in his hands. "Hey," said Captain Edward. "You can walk to the spot Ruth has for you. She said for me to make sure you didn't fall over or something."

Augustus sighed, not even looking up. "I might," he mumbled.

Captain Edward paused, his eyebrows furrowing deeper. "Alright," he answered, trying to hide his nervousness. "Just stand up and I'll do my best to hold you up." He held his hand out.

Augustus heaved another deep sigh, reaching for Captain Edward's hand. With much effort, he slowly pulled himself to his feet, immediately wobbling dramatically. Captain Edward caught Augustus by the shoulders and helped him regain his balance. They slowly walked out into the hallway.

As they turned the corner, Augustus lost his balance, nearly toppling them both over. Ruth glanced over, and her eyes widened. This was getting a little scary. How could a grown man have suddenly become so weak? Ruth swallowed hard. Few things scared her worse than the possibility of someone else's life being in danger. What if Augustus got worse?

Captain Edward's expression was getting more serious by the minute. "Stephan," he puffed, "Get over here and help me. I didn't realize he was this weak."

Stephan dropped what he was doing and hurried over. He grabbed one of Augustus's shoulders and Captain Edward took the other. They supported him for the last few steps into the mess room.

Augustus sank onto the nearest bed. Captain Edward and Stephan turned to see Jonas watching from the mess room doorway. Deep concern was etched across his weary face. Obviously, Jonas wasn't as weak as Augustus, since he had walked to the door by himself; but he seemed rightfully concerned about Augustus.

Jonas sat down on the bed lined up next to Augustus's. Ruth summoned her courage, walked into the mess room, and knelt next to Augustus. Although few things scared her worse, few situations made her want to help more. She tugged the blanket out from underneath him. "Alright," she said. "You can lie down now."

Augustus slowly lowered himself until he was sprawled out over the tiny bed. Ruth pulled up the covers from under his feet and gently pulled them up to his chin. Augustus took a deep breath and closed his eyes.

Ruth quietly stood up and walked to the galley to grab the rag. Returning to Augustus's bed, she gently laid it across his forehead. Augustus's eyes opened.

"I'm just putting this on your forehead to help with your fever," Ruth said in a reassuring voice.

Augustus closed his eyes again, and after Ruth put a rag on Jonas's forehead, she walked to her room and found another rag. Quietly, she crept back down the hall, grabbed the water-filled bucket from the galley, and tiptoed up the stairs to the top deck.

"Clean the rails," she mused to herself. She plopped the rag into the bucket, swished it around, and squeezed it out. She then set to work scrubbing the handrails. The first time she pulled the rag off the rails to look at it, her nose turned up. Layers of dust and dirt were streaked across its surface. "Ew," she muttered. "He was right. These rails *are* disgusting!"

First Mate Leonard walked by, and Ruth flashed him a smile. "See?" she said with a twinkle in her eye. "I remembered!"

"What?"

"The rails. You asked me to clean them."

"Oh," was all Leonard said. He really wasn't much for words today, which contributed to Ruth's thinking he wasn't feeling well.

Leonard walked away, and Ruth began singing rather loudly. "O worship the king, all glorious above, O gratefully sing — oh, wait a minute," she corrected herself. "I don't want to wake up the men below deck." Ruth lowered her voice and began singing more quietly. She listened as the men talked nearby.

"We're going to have a harder time finding our bearings without Augustus," Captain Edward sighed. "When you're disoriented and your sailing master comes down sick, you're in trouble."

Leonard nodded. "I agree."

"I suppose we'll continue the procedures for deduced reckoning and hope he's back up soon," Captain Edward decided. The others nodded and walked away.

The day seemed to drag by. Ruth slowly but surely worked at the rails, and now and then she'd check on the sick sailors and bring them whatever they might need. After the midday meal, she checked on them again and re-soaked the little cloths she kept on their foreheads. It was work, but taking care of people was one thing Ruth loved to do.

When the sun was beginning to sink in the west, Augustus and Jonas weren't much better. Neither was Sean, who upon waking up, had realized he wasn't any more up for getting back to work than they were. And, as the day had dragged on, Alan's headache had gotten worse and worse until he too was confined to his bed. It was like the galley had become a miniature hospital.

As evening shadows gradually gave way to moonlit darkness, Ruth made sure the sick sailors had what they needed for the night.

"I'll be back in a few hours," Ruth whispered softly, "to check on you. Good night." Offering them one last smile, she slipped away to her own room.

"Please, God," she prayed. "Help them get well again. I want them to be alright!" With that heartfelt prayer, Ruth slipped into bed and closed her own weary eyes.

Let love be without hypocrisy...Be devoted to one another in brotherly love...not lagging behind in diligence, fervent in spirit, serving the Lord; rejoicing in hope, persevering in tribulation, devoted to prayer, contributing to the needs of the saints, practicing hospitality.

Free

*Bless those who persecute you; bless and do
not curse. Never pay back evil for evil to
anyone. Respect what is right in the sight of
all men. If possible, so far as it depends on
you, be at peace with all men. Never take
your own revenge... "But if your enemy is
hungry, feed him, and if he is thirsty, give
him a drink..." Do not be overcome by evil,
but overcome evil with good.*

(Romans 12:9-14, 17-20 NASB)

Careena Campbell

Free

Chapter Eight

How Firm A Foundation

For no man can lay a foundation other than that which is laid, which is Jesus Christ.

(1 Corinthians 3:11 NASB)

*R*uth's eyes opened. Moonlight cast little shapes onto the walls and floor of the tiny room. Well, she had probably been asleep for a while now. It was time to check on the sick sailors.

Sleepily Ruth rolled out of bed and tiptoed into the hall. A floorboard creaked as she stepped into the mess room, and Alan's eyes opened.

"Hello," Ruth whispered softly. "Do you need anything?"

In the next room over, Captain Edward stirred. He could faintly hear Ruth's soft voice. In an instant, he was fully awake. Ruth had gotten up and was taking care of them again. It seemed so out-of-place, even almost wrong. A young girl, captive on a ship, sacrificing sleep and risking her own health to help the very men she had wrongly been forced to call her masters. But that wasn't the only thing keeping Captain Edward awake. Deep in his heart, he had a distressing feeling. Ruth could take risks like that because she had given her life to God, and she trusted Him to take care of her. But Captain Edward hadn't given God his trust, and suddenly, it seemed real. Too real. So real it was too frightening to bear.

Captain Edward was too riled up to go back to sleep now, so he slipped out of his bunk and stood in his cabin doorway watching Ruth.

Ruth tended to Augustus, Jonas, Sean, and Alan as they lay on their beds and cots. She gently put her hand to Alan's hot brow, then pulled a rag from a bowl of water and placed it on his forehead.

"Well," Ruth whispered to herself, "the Bible says God is 'a very present help in trouble'. There's a psalm somewhere where the psalmist is praying to God during his sickness. Guess we'll have to do the same."

Talking about Scriptures helped Ruth not feel so creeped out by the eerie lantern-lit shadows. It also helped her stay encouraged about the situation. The day's work had tired her, and now she was up in the middle of the night. But it was worth it. Such a sacrifice was just what she felt God wanted her to do.

Leonard appeared at the end of the hallway. Just one quick glance told Ruth he was ill. His weathered face was flushed, and he looked like he desperately needed to rest.

"Low food, low water, sick, and lost," he grumbled. "What more could go wrong?"

Before Captain Edward had time to even think about how to respond, Ruth offered a positive answer. "Well, it must be God's will, so I guess we'll have to accept it."

"I can't possibly accept something so bad," Leonard objected. "Besides, I thought God would give people *good* things."

"Oh, He does!" Ruth exclaimed. "Romans 8:28 says, 'And we know that all things work together for good to them that love God, to them who are the called

Free

according to *his* purpose.' Even good things don't always feel good at first."

"And...and what if we don't love God?" Captain Edward asked anxiously.

Ruth thought for a moment. "Well, God gives blessings to everyone. But in the end, only people who have made Him their Savior go to heaven. And as much as he wants people to love Him, He doesn't *make* them love Him."

"Because with as wonderful as you make God out to be, it seems we could never, ever love Him as much as He loves us."

"Well, we can't. None of us can," Ruth explained. "But the little bit of love you can give is exactly what He wants you to give Him. He knows you aren't perfect. But that's why He sent Jesus."

Captain Edward nodded, then looked up to see Leonard was already walking back down the hallway. "Leonard," Captain Edward called quietly, "seriously. You really ought to take a break and get some sleep."

First Mate Leonard cast him a sour look. "Somebody has to fill in for the sick men," he grumbled, and he disappeared down the hall.

Ruth and Captain Edward sighed at the same time. Leonard was obviously not well, but was his pride keeping him from getting the rest he needed? Ruth knew controlling Leonard was not her responsibility, so she said a silent prayer for him and kept caring for the sick sailors around her.

Ruth looked up at Captain Edward. By the anxious look on his face, it seemed he had a lot on his mind. When Ruth left to hoist up more water, Captain Edward didn't even seem to notice her. His eyes were fixed to the floor, and his thoughts seemed to be in a place far away.

What Ruth couldn't see was that Captain Edward was struggling through a sea of thoughts. *You've stood aloof instead of dressing them down,* his thoughts hissed. *You're a failure as a leader.*

On the top deck, Ruth yawned and shook her head in an effort to stay awake. A fresh breeze blew into her face as she stepped onto the top deck. Oh, that felt nice. Maybe that would help her stay awake. She was *so* sleepy, but knowing God had given her the job of caring for these men gave her all the motivation he needed to stay up.

Ruth's thoughts were foggy, and she moved slowly as she hoisted the bucket up from the water. She kept her mind occupied by pondering all the things that seemed to have changed.

Ruth realized life on this ship was not as frightening for her as it used to be. She wondered why. It couldn't just be that the sailors weren't as harsh with her now, or that she'd tried hard enough to stay positive. It was just that God had given her peace. Peace in knowing what? Peace in seeing each situation as the current place God had placed her in. And that if God had placed her there, it was where she belonged. Ruth cringed at the thought of belonging on this ship forever. For now, since God had allowed her to be here, it was where she belonged. Her job was to be open to His will.

With a contented feeling, Ruth carried the water down the stairs and set the bucket beside Sean's bed. She gently lifted the rag off his forehead and re-soaked it before putting it back in its place.

"Alright," Ruth whispered, "I'll go now so you can all go back to sleep."

Free

Ruth stood up and turned to Captain Edward, Hector, and Alessio, who were standing nearby. "Would you all care for a snack?" she asked quietly.

Alessio nodded. "Aye."

"Alright," Ruth agreed. "I'll meet you on the deck." She quietly grabbed some meat and sea biscuits from the galley. She placed them on a tray before tiptoeing through the corridor and up the stairs to the top deck. "You guys want to break for a snack?" she offered to the watchmen.

Charles, Theodore, and First Mate Leonard exchanged glances.

"I've got to man the lookout," Charles answered.

"Alright," Theodore nodded, his shoulder-length black hair falling in his eyes. "And then I'll man it so you can grab a bite to eat and get some shuteye."

"Sounds fine."

First Mate Leonard and Theodore walked over to Ruth, joining Captain Edward and Alessio. After the men picked up their portions, Ruth went below deck to fetch some mugs and fill them with water. When she came back, she offered them to the men.

"No, thanks," Leonard objected, raising a hand. Shadows shivered across his pale face in the moonlight.

Ruth looked confused. "But you —"

"We don't have much," First Mate Leonard persisted.

Ruth hesitated, but then nodded obediently. "Alright." She moved on, passing out mugs to the others. After that, the midnight silence took over.

Everyone seemed quieter, at least it felt that way in the dark. Captain Edward was particularly silent. His face was like a dark cloud as he stared down at his biscuits. Ruth wondered what was wrong. She prayed silently, asking God to help him with whatever he was going through.

Captain Edward continued to circle in his drowning thoughts. *You've chosen fear over courage,* taunted his thoughts. *What kind of man are you?*

After their snack, the men went their separate ways. Ruth heaved a weary sigh, placing the dishes in a stack on the table. As long as the sick sailors didn't need anything more, she could go back to bed after the cleanup.

Washing the dishes could wait until tomorrow, Ruth decided, setting the last mug on the stack. Finally, she could go back to bed and get rest for the next day.

Turning to leave, Ruth nearly crashed into Captain Edward. They walked by each other, but then Ruth heard his voice: "Ruth…"

Ruth turned around. "Yes?"

Captain Edward seemed hesitant. "Were you going to bed?"

Ruth examined his face. His eyebrows were furrowed, like he was worried about something.

"Yes," Ruth answered in response to his question.

"Alright, then." Captain Edward turned away and continued down the hall.

Ruth took two steps forward, but then turned back. "Did you need something?"

Captain Edward turned around again. It seemed as if he were trying to make up his mind about something. Looking up at Ruth, he asked, "Do you have a moment?"

Ruth hesitated. She really wanted to go back to bed, but that would be selfish. How often did the captain pull her aside like this? On that note, what if this was a trap? Nonsense. Captain Edward had never done anything to harm her, and she didn't expect him to start now. As long as they wouldn't be by themselves, Ruth decided she would see what he needed.

Ruth nodded slowly. "Of course."

"Here," whispered Captain Edward, "let's go to the top deck so we won't disturb anyone." He walked in a straight line down the hall and swiftly scaled the stairs. Ruth breathed a sigh of relief. The top deck would be safe—out in the open and near other people. Limping down the hall, she followed him.

All was still above deck. The clouds hung silently. The sea was calm. Even the wind had ceased to blow. The floor hardly even creaked as Captain Edward walked to the ship's edge.

Ruth felt goosebumps on her skin as she followed him. Not that she was afraid, but the midnight chill and the waves of anticipation made her shiver. She stood quietly beside Captain Edward, waiting for him to continue.

Captain Edward leaned on the railing. He gazed out over the ocean, stroking his beard. He swallowed hard.

Ruth held her breath in anticipation.

Finally, Captain Edward reached into the pocket of his coat and pulled out the Bible, the one Ruth had found.

"I've been reading this."

Ruth gasped, her face broadening into a smile.

"I know I've done wrong things," Captain Edward continued. "When hanging out with the others, I've done things I shouldn't have. I just never had a solid reason to say no. I didn't have something to set the standard for right and wrong; a reason to tell them they shouldn't do something. Even though I felt some things were wrong, that wasn't enough for them to listen. That's why when you showed up here, I didn't make them take you back. I knew that would be the right thing, but if I said so, they would ask me why. And I knew I wouldn't have a good enough answer. So, I didn't do what was right." In his head, his thoughts hissed again: *You see? You're a failure as a leader.* It seemed so loud, he had to say it out loud: "I've been a failure as a leader." He shook his head and stared again at the sea, blinking back tears. *Oh God, help me understand,* he prayed through the thoughts.

Ruth listened with wide eyes. For a moment, she didn't know what to say. Finally, she whispered, "But God can free you from all that. He can help you be strong, and as you've realized, His Word is the truth that you can ground your beliefs in. When His Holy Spirit comes into your life, He gives you strength to stand up for the truths in His Word."

"I know. I know it does," Captain Edward answered, nodding. "My parents used to tell me about all that—about Jesus…and His death on the cross…and how it could somehow pay for sins. But it never seemed real. Now it does. I know it's real." He paused and looked her in the eyes. "I know because I've seen it in you."

Ruth's jaw dropped, and her heart flooded with joy. *He's seen God in me!* she thought. Ruth momentarily felt as though she would cry with happiness.

Captain Edward's heart, though, was still wrestling with his doubts. A look of concern shadowed his face as he spoke aloud the lie that had been echoing in his mind: "But, I mean, are you sure God *wants* me?"

Ruth looked deep into his face and leaned forward. "Captain Edward," she said, "He *died* for you. What more could He do to show He wants you?"

Captain Edward sighed and nodded. The troubled thoughts began clearing at the truth, like a ray of light piercing a cloud. A small smile began creeping onto his face. "I know. And I'm ready to accept that. I'm ready to accept Jesus as my Savior." He looked at Ruth. "Would you help me?"

For a moment, Ruth couldn't speak because she was too overwhelmed with joy. "I would love nothing more!" she exclaimed. She reached toward Captain Edward's Bible. "May I read you something?"

"Please." Captain Edward, now relaxing, handed her the Bible. Ruth flipped to Romans and found the verse her parents had often used to lead people to Christ.

"Here," she urged, holding the Bible where Captain Edward could see it. "Read this verse."

Captain Edward looked where she was pointing. He read aloud, "'That if thou shalt confess with thy mouth the Lord Jesus, and shalt believe in thine heart that God hath raised him from the dead, thou shalt be saved. For with the heart man believeth unto righteousness; and with the mouth confession is made unto salvation. For the Scripture saith, Whoever believeth on him shall not be ashamed.'"

Ruth looked into Captain Edward's face. "Do you believe that God has raised Jesus from the dead?"

"Yes," Captain Edward answered. "And I believe that Jesus is Lord. From now on He will be Lord of my life."

Ruth's face illuminated with joy. "Well, then, you're saved! Let's pray!"

Captain Edward's smile filled his face. "Should I kneel?"

"If you want to."

Captain Edward and Ruth knelt together. "Lord Jesus," Captain Edward prayed, "thank You for giving everything for me. I now give You my life, my heart, my love, my praise...everything. Do with it what You want. Amen."

Captain Edward opened his eyes, and a tear of joy slipped onto his cheek. His broad smile was reflected onto Ruth's face.

"HUZZAH!" Ruth half-shouted. "Praise the Lord!" She and Captain Edward burst out laughing together.

"...What's going on over here?" interrupted a deep voice.

Captain Edward and Ruth looked up to see several of the night watchmen standing in front of them.

Captain Edward stood up, and Ruth stood up behind him. "He's my brother!" she proclaimed victoriously.

"*What?*" Stephan looked very confused.

"Well," Captain Edward chuckled nervously. "She means figuratively speaking."

"Huh?" Theodore didn't get it.

Ruth grinned. "He just accepted Jesus as his Savior!"

114

Captain Edward smiled at Ruth, but the others didn't look pleased. They exchanged unhappy glances. "What's that going to mean?" wondered Theodore.

"It means I'm serving God now," Captain Edward answered. "And it also means there are going to be some changes on this ship."

Stephan narrowed his eyes. "Like what?"

"Well," Captain Edward began, "First of all, I'm going to be putting some evening rules in place. There's no wrong in having fun, but I think we can all agree our rowdy late-night craziness has been going too far."

"Are you joking!" Stephan sputtered. "We're sailors! What do you think you can make this place, a church? This—"

Captain Edward stepped up to Stephan and looked him square in the face. "Don't you talk back to me. What is right is right, whether you agree or not."

Leonard glared at Captain Edward. "I don't like this. You want to be religious, that's fine; but you don't have to—"

"You don't have to like it," interrupted Captain Edward. His voice was firm. "I'm doing it because that's what God asks of me."

Stephan started to step toward Ruth, glaring. "What did you do to him?" he yelled.

Ruth gasped, her eyes widening. How could someone be angry over such a good thing? "I—!" she protested.

Ruth felt Captain Edward take her arm and gently urge her to step back. Ruth obediently stepped back as Captain Edward pushed Stephan away from her. "Don't you even think about hurting her!" he ordered.

"She did nothing. It was the saving power of Jesus Christ that changed me!"

The others looked stunned. What on earth had just happened to their captain? They exchanged glances. First Mate Leonard was the one to step up to Captain Edward. "Fine. You can do what you like. But don't be surprised if a few of your crewmen's contracts end a little early." With that, he stomped off. The others followed.

Captain Edward sighed, then looked down at Ruth. She was a little stunned, but quickly recovered. "That was awesome!" she sputtered.

Captain Edward's smile returned. "Thank you."

"You're already standing up for what's right," Ruth smiled. "Praise Jesus!"

Captain Edward nodded. "Aye." His gaze, however, quickly shifted to his unhappy crewmen across the deck.

"They just don't know what you know," Ruth said quietly, as if reading his thoughts. "I pray that they will someday. You did what was right."

The assurance in her voice reminded Captain Edward of why he had done what he had. He smiled and began to walk away, then turned back. He knew his crew was going to be questioning his new rules, so he wanted to have some Scripture under his belt.

"Ruth," he asked quietly, "does the Bible say anything about staying up late being, well…rowdy?"

Ruth thought a moment. "Umm…yes, somewhere in Galatians, I think. It says Christians shouldn't be doing 'revelry', or rowdy partying — if that's what you mean."

Captain Edward nodded and held up his Bible. "Perfect. I'll see if I can look it up. Thank you, Ruth." As he walked away, he hummed. He knew in his heart serving Jesus would be worth it, no matter the resistance from his crew.

Ruth joined his tune in a soft, beautiful song:

"How firm a foundation, ye saints of the Lord,

Is laid for your faith in His excellent word!

What more can He say then to you He hath said,

To you who for refuge to Jesus hath fled!"

Careena Campbell

Chapter Nine

Where I Belong

Let love of the brethren continue.

(Hebrews 13:1 NASB)

*R*uth rolled over groggily. She knew it was probably morning, but she was still so sleepy.

Suddenly, her eyes popped open. Her heart leaped. Oh! Captain Edward was saved now! This was a day to rejoice! Ruth sat up, her face gleaming, and read her Bible. She then limped out of the room and down the hall. She passed the mess room quietly, deciding to let the sick sailors rest a little longer. Up she headed to the top deck.

Captain Edward was already on the sterncastle, watching as Charles, Hector, and Alessio went about their morning routines. Ruth limped over to him with a skip in her step. "GOOD morning!" she exclaimed rather loudly.

"Oh!" Captain Edward gasped, laughing, as if her sudden presence startled him. "Good morning."

Ruth's eyes sparkled. "This is the day the Lord has made, let us rejoice and be glad in it!"

Captain Edward grinned. "Is that a Bible verse?"

"Yes," replied Ruth. "I don't remember the exact reference, but it's in the Psalms somewhere."

"Alright," Captain Edward answered. Chuckling, he added, "I really need to memorize some

Bible verses. You're always quoting Scriptures, and I want to be able to, too."

"Well," Ruth shrugged, "it's never too late! I've been reading my Bible since the time I could read. I read it every morning and evening. If you do that, too, I bet you'll be surprised how often the Holy Spirit brings to mind the Scriptures you've read."

"If you say so," agreed Captain Edward. "I guess I'll start doing that. I'm just glad I can read. Not everybody can. I suppose they'd have to wait until someone had time to read them the Bible. That'd be rough. Where'd you learn to read?" Captain Edward wondered.

Ruth felt a tug on her heart. "Well, my mom couldn't read, so she asked some of the missionary women to teach me how. And my papa helped. I used to read over his shoulder at Bible time."

Captain Edward glanced at her, raising his eyebrows in surprise. "Missionary women?"

"Yes," Ruth answered. "Missionary women."

Captain Edward nodded, and for a moment, he and Ruth stood in the warm sunshine. Afterwards, Ruth decided to move on with her day. "Well," she said, "I'd better go check on the sick ones."

"Alright," answered Captain Edward. "I don't want to tie you up."

"Alright!" Ruth skipped across the deck to the stairs.

Across the deck, Charles watched her go, then watched as Captain Edward pulled out the ship's logbook and began writing. "Probably about last night," Charles mused. "Did you hear about what happened?" he whispered to Hector and Alessio.

"No," Hector answered.

"Edward got religious," Charles said. "And he also said we can't be rowdy at night anymore. He told me it was against the Bible."

Alessio looked disappointed. "Oh...but we enjoy doing that! I mean, come on—all sailors do it."

"I know," Charles nodded. "I mean, he's captain and can do what he wants, but it's still a bummer."

"Who told you about this?" asked Hector.

"Leonard did," replied Charles. "And he didn't seem very happy about it."

"I can imagine," Alessio agreed. "Leonard doesn't like getting orders from anyone."

Charles watched Captain Edward for a moment. "God's just so real to them," he mused.

Alessio glanced over. "What do you mean?"

"Well, I grew up going to church," Charles explained. "But when I moved out of the house, I quit on it. It just felt like it was more rituals than relationship. I mean, I acknowledge God *exists,* but not in the same way they do. With Ruth and Captain Edward it's different. They talk about God being a loyal, loving...Friend. They say He cares about everyone on a deep, personal level."

Alessio nodded. "I know what you mean."

Meanwhile, down below deck, Ruth stepped into the mess room. "Good morning," she greeted. "How are you guys doing? I see you're sitting up, Augustus. Less dizzy today, I take it?"

"Aye," Augustus said with a smile. "Much better, thank you."

Jonas propped himself on his elbow. "I might be able to get up and around a little today."

"Me too," echoed Sean.

"Good!" Ruth exclaimed happily. "I've been praying for you. How's your headache, Alan?"

Alan winced. "Mm, it's there. Not as bad, though. Maybe I'll be able to get back to work."

"Oh, I would be careful," Ruth cautioned. "If you work yourselves too hard now, you'll feel worse later."

The men nodded reluctantly, and Ruth heard Hector's voice behind her: "Señorita Ruth?"

Ruth turned around. "Sí, Hector?"

Hector coughed into his elbow, then blinked. "Are they doing better?"

Ruth nodded. "Yes, very much."

"So, should I take them off the binnacle list?"

Ruth glanced at the men. Alan stood up. "You can take me off." With that, he left the room.

Ruth sighed under her breath. She'd just told him to rest! Oh, well. Alan was probably alright. "Alan can," Ruth agreed. "But I wouldn't take the others off yet."

Hector nodded and scribbled into his logbook. He then looked up to see Captain Edward standing in the doorway.

"Are they doing alright?" asked Captain Edward.

Hector nodded, leaning on the wall. "Yes, captain, but I think…"

Ruth glanced at Hector. He was slumped against the wall and looked tired. *Oh, no,* Ruth thought. *Oh, no.*

Captain Edward seemed to realize it too. "Are you ill, Hector?"

Hector hesitated. "Perhaps. I just needed your permission to…to put me on the list."

"Of course," Captain Edward nodded. "Of course."

"Alright. Thank you. I'm sorry, I just—"

"Don't fret over it."

Hector sank onto the bed that had been Alan's and half-heartedly scratched his name into the binnacle list. Ruth felt a tinge of panic. "Hector!" she exclaimed, trying to be quiet. "What will I do without you? I mean, what if something goes wrong?"

"The others are fine now. Just keep doing what you're doing. You seem to have a skill for it; a woman's touch, perhaps."

Ruth was surprised by his compliment. She may have been His instrument, but God had healed the men. "Oh, it's not me!" she stammered.

"It's the great God we serve," finished Captain Edward, pausing as he walked up the hall.

Ruth smiled at him, and Sean cocked his head. "What do you mean, 'we'?"

"I'm a follower of God now," Captain Edward explained. "And He's a great Healer, isn't He, Ruth?"

Ruth smiled. "Yes. He sure is."

Hector stood up, paused, and began shuffling out of the room. "Do you need me to fetch you anything? Here, take this." Ruth held out a damp rag for Hector to put on his forehead.

Hector held out his hand to stop her. "I'll be fine," he said, although his eyes looked like he was lightheaded. "You just take care of the others and I'll take care of myself." With that, Hector left.

Ruth sat quietly for a moment. "Well," she said finally, "I'd better be getting on with my work," She stood up. "Don't forget to keep drinking water, and thank Jesus! He's really been watching out for you." With that, she disappeared down the hall and into her room.

The sailors watched with a smile. Ruth's cheerfulness was contagious — even a rugged sailor had a hard time resisting a smile when she was around. But Captain Edward's smile was probably the biggest. He chuckled fondly as he returned to his work.

In the tiny room down the hall, Ruth shuffled through the stacks of items that were being stored there. As she peered around a barrel, she spied a long wooden handle. She pulled it out, revealing a tassel of thick rope at the other end.

"Aha!" Ruth declared. "I figured they had to have a mop somewhere."

After she had hauled up some seawater, Ruth set to work. Adjusting her stance so she could get the most leverage out of her legs, she plopped the mop onto the floor and scrubbed. As she worked, she hummed.

After a few feet of floor were thoroughly wet, Ruth rinsed out the mop. Swirls of dirty brown marred the blue water in the bucket. Wow, this floor was filthy. She was going to need to change the water quite frequently.

Free

As Ruth set back to scrubbing, she suddenly realized how tired she was. Her eyes were heavy, and her body felt weary. Of course, it was to be expected after getting up in the middle of the night after a hard day's work.

I wouldn't trade it for the world, Ruth thought with a warm heart. *It's a good witness, and Captain Edward placed his faith in Jesus. That's worth* anything!

Still, as Ruth looked up at the stretch of floor spread out before her, she wondered how long it would take and how many breaks she'd need.

As she was about to look back down at the floor in front of her, Ruth noticed First Mate Leonard standing not far from her. He was leaning on the railing, breathing heavy. His face looked another shade paler and creased in an uncomfortable expression. Ruth looked at him in concern. How far was he going to push himself before resting? Compassion stirred in Ruth's heart. With the mop still in her hand, she limped over to him.

"Excuse me, Master Leonard," she said timidly. "Are you alright?"

First Mate Leonard frowned. "How many times am I going to have to tell you? I'm fine!" he snapped. He turned around so fast he bumped his shoulder into Ruth's face. Caught off-guard, Ruth wobbled on her short leg. "Would you quit trying to take care of me?" He batted at the mop in her hand, and Ruth fell over on her short leg.

A blur passed in front of Ruth as a man shoved Leonard away from her. Ruth recognized him as Captain Edward. His mouth was set in a straight line, and Ruth realized she had never seen Captain Edward so angry before.

Captain Edward stood between Ruth and Leonard. He stood up straight, his shoulders squared. Leonard was taller, but Captain Edward's figure dominated as he sternly addressed Leonard: "I *said* no one was to touch her!"

For a moment, Leonard stared at him with a stunned expression. Dumbfounded, he stammered, "But I just—"

"Don't do that again," Captain Edward commanded. "If you do, there will be serious consequences."

Tension hung. Leonard looked frustrated. Ruth tried to make herself look small as she sat on the deck floor. *Uh oh,* she thought, scooting several feet back. *Are they about to get in a fight over this?*

Leonard opened his mouth, but then stopped. With a reluctant sigh, Leonard nodded. "Aye, sir."

Captain Edward stepped away, and Leonard quickly disappeared down the stairs into the hull. Captain Edward stepped over to Ruth and helped her up. "Ruth," he said seriously, "if he does that again, you come and get me."

Ruth nodded, but she sure hoped that wouldn't happen again. "Yes, sir."

With a frustrated sigh, Captain Edward walked away. Across the deck, Hector's jaw dropped. "Did you see *that*?" he gasped.

Charles nodded in amazement. "Edward got an 'aye, sir' out of Leonard! When's the last time Leonard showed that much respect?"

Alessio shook his head. "I don't even remember. A long time ago—way back before Edward started letting Leonard have his way around here. That had to be at least two years ago."

126

"Well," Charles sighed, "at least Edward is standing up for himself again. Seems as if he expected someone else to do the dressing down for him — which of course ended up being Leonard."

Alessio nodded. "Aye."

Meanwhile, Ruth had gone back to mopping. A smile spread across her face.

"Now I don't just have a sailor making rules to protect me," she thought, beaming. "Now Captain Edward is ready and willing to get in there and protect me." Ruth's heart spun happy circles. Any girl loves to feel protected. "It makes me feel safe. Wow. It's been a long time since I could say that." Ruth's tiredness pulled a sad tug at her heart, but she swept a stray hair off her face and scrubbed the floor a little harder.

A short while later, Ruth was dumping out the little bucket, and Captain Edward walked by.

Ruth straightened up. "Captain Edward!"

Captain Edward halted his steps. "What?"

Ruth hesitated. She felt a little shy saying this, but she wanted to anyway. "Thank you."

"For what?"

"For protecting me. It's, well, been a long time since I had a man who did that for me."

Captain Edward chuckled. "It's my pleasure, Ruth. Any time you need me, I'm here."

Ruth's face glowed, and she went back to mopping. "Thank you."

The day passed rather slowly. Nothing exciting happened that demanded attention from the crews. Alan, Sean, Augustus, and Jonas spent most of the day resting, but they were able to get up and around some.

Augustus was even able to help Captain Edward in continuing to try and figure out the ship's location. And throughout the day, the span of unmopped floor steadily shrunk until, finally, as night was falling, Ruth stood with satisfaction on the bow.

"There," she said, gazing out at the now-mopped deck. "That makes me feel good." She reached down to rinse out the mop one last time. She was so tired that it felt like it took a lot of effort just to squeeze out the mophead.

Ruth picked up the bucket and slowly dumped it into the ocean. As Ruth listened to the merry bubbling of the water falling into the sea, she thought she'd sing along with its tune.

"I am a poor wayfaring stranger," she sang softly,

"Traveling through this world below.

There is no sickness, toil, or danger

In that bright world to which I go.

"I'm going there to see my Father,

I'm going there no more to roam.

I am just going over Jordan.

I am just going home."

Ruth sighed with satisfaction, wiping sweat from her brow. "Yes," she whispered. "This world is not my home. God's given me places to belong in the meantime, but someday in heaven I'll *really* belong!"

Ruth's face held a happy smile as she walked across the deck. Just before reaching the stairs, Ruth turned around for one last view of the nice clean deck.

But just as she turned to leave, Ruth's serene moment was suddenly interrupted. First Mate Leonard was walking across the deck—much slower than she'd ever seen.

Ruth snapped to attention. Something was wrong. Leonard breathed heavily and shut his eyes tight. He reached out a shaking hand to lean on the mast, looking like he was about to fall over.

Ruth's eyes widened. Something was VERY wrong! She began running toward him as best as she could. "Master Leonard! Are you—"

Suddenly, Leonard exhaled and collapsed into a heap—unconscious.

Ruth stopped dead in her tracks, slapping her hand over her mouth to keep from screaming. She wasn't sure what to do, so she yelled for someone who would: "Captain Edward, get up here, NOW!"

She was hardly finished with her sentence when Captain Edward bolted up the stairs. "What happened?"

Ruth's voice trembled. "I—I—Leonard—he—"

Captain Edward peered around her and gasped to see Leonard lying on the floor. He ran to join two other sailors who had gathered next to Leonard.

This just seemed too much. Should she help? Ruth felt uncharacteristically frozen. Was it the effect of hard work and lack of sleep or a fear for what was wrong with Leonard? She turned away, trying to calm herself as her heart hammered.

She listened to the men's voices: "What happened?" said someone.

"I don't know," came Captain Edward's voice. "Ruth screamed, so I ran up."

"Where's Hector?" asked someone.

"He's —" Captain Edward glanced around, then suddenly remembered. "Hector's ill. Ruth!"

Captain Edward was calling for her. Ruth's heart hammered. Why was she so afraid? Was she afraid of what she would see? Was she afraid Leonard was dying? Was she just tired and stressed?

Captain Edward needs me, Ruth thought. *Leonard needs me. I need to obey Captain Edward.* Ruth swallowed her fears, willed to not start crying, and limped over to where Leonard was lying. Theodore was sitting next to Leonard beside Captain Edward, and a sailor Ruth didn't recognize stood on the other side.

Ruth wasn't sure where she should start. She wasn't supposed to touch Leonard much, so how would she check his condition or figure out what had happened? She decided to first ask what her mother had always asked about an unconscious person: "Is he breathing?"

"Yes," came the answer.

Ruth nodded. That was what was most important. Next, she needed clues as to why Leonard had passed out. She'd already been suspicious he had a fever, so she should check that. That was something she could do without touching him too much. But she'd have to be right next to the sailors around Leonard. Timidly, Ruth walked over to where Captain Edward was and knelt beside him. Cautiously, she held out her hand and felt Leonard's forehead. It was burning with fever.

Ruth recalled that Leonard had refused to take very long rest breaks. She remembered how he'd turned down a drink of water. *Of course,* Ruth thought. *Of course he passed out, with a fever like this and beating his body up like that.*

"I think he'll be alright," Ruth told the others. "He just pushed himself too hard."

"Should we get him below deck?" suggested Theodore.

"That would be a good idea," Ruth agreed.

Ruth stood back as the Theodore and the other sailor picked Leonard up and carried him below deck. It was a little spooky to see Leonard's long, strong body so limp. Emotion started welling up in her again. She tried to remain calm as she limped behind Captain Edward toward the hatch, but she felt her chest start to shake.

Captain Edward glanced behind him to make sure Ruth was still with him. He did a double take, seeing her face. "Ruth," he said quietly, stopping. "Are you alright?"

Ruth shook her head as a signal she didn't want to talk about it. She didn't want to break down in front of him. She trusted him, but she didn't want to be that vulnerable. Besides, other sailors might be nearby, and she knew they'd stare at her.

"What's wrong?" Captain Edward continued.

Captain Edward's voice was so calm, so gentle, and so thoughtful. But it was how much it reminded her of her father's that made Ruth feel like the wall inside her was crumbling. A tear spilled out of each of her eyes.

"I'm just—" Ruth's voice broke. Against her will, tears started trickling down her cheeks. Embarrassment jabbed her. "I'm sorry!" she apologized. "I'm sorry, I just—I'm tired, I'm a little stressed, I'm worried about Leonard..." Ruth had to pause as her voice choked off into a few broken sobs.

Captain Edward felt sorry for her. He understood, as best as a man like him could. She was a tired young woman, and the last few minutes had been intense — especially for a girl who cared as much for people as Ruth did. Captain Edward put his hands on Ruth's slender shoulders. When she felt his strong hands around her tensed shoulders, Ruth choked out a few more sobs.

"It'll be alright," Captain Edward answered calmly. "I think Leonard will be fine. But we could use your help." His gentle voice helped to calm Ruth's pounding heart.

Ruth took a deep breath. She knew she had to be brave and face what came her way. "I'll come," she agreed. She knew God had promised He would never send her more than she could handle.

Captain Edward walked with Ruth down the stairs. Ruth slipped on her short leg, but Captain Edward caught her. Together they walked to the mess room.

Theodore and the other sailor had laid Leonard in the bed that had been Alan's. Alan stood nearby.

"He's coming around," Alan said to Captain Edward.

"Good," Captain Edward answered. "Ruth," he said, nodding toward Leonard.

Ruth stepped over to Leonard.

Leonard's eyes were only half-open, but he managed to mumble, "No."

"She's going to help you," Charles explained.

Leonard mumbled something else, but Ruth couldn't understand it. She knelt beside him, trying to decide what to do first.

After a few seconds, she pulled up a tent of skin on the back of Leonard's hand. It slowly collapsed back down.

"He's dehydrated," she whispered to herself. She turned to face the others. "Can you please get me drinking water, ocean water, and more rags?"

Captain Edward gave Alan a slight push. "Get them," he instructed.

Alan looked offended. "So. We're following a *slave's* orders, now, huh?"

Captain Edward looked indignant. He gave Alan a pointed look, and Alan and Theodore left to fetch the requested items, and Captain Edward turned back to Ruth. "Where'd you learn all this?" he asked.

Ruth felt Leonard's forehead as she answered, "My mother taught me. She was always helping sick people in the villages we visited. She used to say, 'If someone needs help and you can help them, you should.'" Ruth closed her eyes and shook her head because thinking about her mom made her sad. Trying to think about something else, Ruth began quietly singing "How Firm a Foundation," beginning with verse two:

"When through fiery trials thy pathway shall lie,

My grace, all-sufficient, shall be thy supply.

The flame shall not hurt thee, I only design

Thy dross to consume and thy gold to refine."

Cots creaked. Ruth noticed Augustus, Sean, and Jonas watching her. Her face turned a shade of red. "Did I wake you up?"

"No, no," said Augustus with a small smile.

Ruth turned back to Leonard and began singing in her head.

"Please," urged Captain Edward. "Keep singing."

A startled expression crossed Ruth's face. A smile tugged at the corners of her mouth as she asked, "You mean, you *want* me to sing?"

Captain Edward shrugged. "I enjoy it."

Ruth's eyes sparkled. Turning back to Leonard, she continued quietly:

"When through the deep waters I call thee to go,

The rivers of woe shall not thee overflow.

For I will be with thee, thy troubles to bless,

And to sanctify thee in thy deepest distress."

Theodore and Alan returned with two pails of water and an armful of rags, which they set on the floor. Ruth smiled at the mountain of rags. Perhaps she should have said a *few!* "Thanks," she said gratefully. She took the pail of drinking water and set it by Leonard's bed.

Ruth grabbed a mug from a little table just inside the men's bedroom, beside which was...her Bible. Her heart leaped, but Ruth knew this was not the time to ask to have it back. She dunked the cup into the water and glanced over at Leonard. He had regained consciousness, but he still looked quite ill. "Master Alan, Master Theodore, would you lift him up so he's in a sitting position, please?"

This time, Alan obliged without objecting. He and Theodore grabbed underneath Leonard's shoulders and propped him up against the wall.

Ruth scooted closer to Leonard's bed. His face was red and burning with fever, and Ruth knew he must be miserable. She felt sorry for him. No matter how badly someone had treated her, it hurt her to see anyone so ill. Gently, she laid a damp cloth on his forehead. "First Mate Leonard," she said, "I know you feel dizzy,

134

but I want you to drink this. Your body needs water."
She picked up the mug and held it out to him.

Leonard wouldn't take it. Captain Edward moved to where Leonard could see him and said, "Leonard, listen to her. She's trying to help you."

"No," Leonard mumbled. "Not her. Not after it all."

Inwardly, Ruth wondered if he was thinking what she was thinking—about how he had treated her and now she was serving him. But she wasn't trying to make him feel bad. She just wanted to serve him. "Here," she said, handing the cup to Captain Edward. "Can you get him to take it?"

Captain Edward took the mug, and Ruth stood up. After making sure the others didn't need anything, she slipped down the hall. "I'll get Leonard something to eat," she said over her shoulder.

"Ruth." Captain Edward stood up and walked after her.

Ruth turned around. "Yes?"

"Why don't you go to bed now," Captain Edward offered.

Ruth felt her heart sink. Leonard needed her! "But Leonard—" she objected.

"We will take care of Leonard now," Captain Edward assured her. Noting the dark circles beneath her eyes, he added, "You look like you could use some rest."

"But I want to help…" Ruth had to pause as she was overtaken with a huge yawn.

Captain Edward smiled. "See what I mean? We'll take care of Leonard," he repeated. "Get some rest, Ruth."

Ruth nodded. She limped to her room and yawned again as she crawled into bed. In a heartbeat, Ruth was sound asleep.

Chapter Ten

Concern

Is anyone among you sick? Then… [the church elders]
are to pray for him.

(James 5:14 NASB)

R uth slowly stirred. Her tired eyes briefly glanced about the room. Sunlight streamed in through the tiny window. Ruth sighed heavily. Oh, dear. That meant she should probably be getting up. But, oh, she didn't want to. After working hard by day and tending to the sick sailors by night, Ruth was thoroughly exhausted. On one hand, she hoped her sacrifice was a good witness for Christ to them; but at the same time, Ruth hoped she would be able to find the energy just to face the day.

Ruth crawled out of bed. Her body ached. As she dragged herself down the hall, the rocking of the ship seemed to taunt her aching stomach. Ruth hoped it was just her exhaustion and not that she was sick.

As she stumbled up the stairs and into the warm sunlight, Ruth realized she'd forgotten to make breakfast. Suppressing a groan, she meandered back down the stairs.

As she passed the mess rook, she noticed that the sick men's beds were empty — well, except for First Mate Leonard's. He was still in bed, but he looked like he was feeling much better. Upon seeing Ruth, he sat up.

"Good morning," Ruth greeted, forcing a smile despite her weariness. "How are you doing this morning?"

Leonard looked at her thoughtfully. He then stood up, as if to leave the room. "Better. Thank you."

"Where are you going?" Ruth asked. "I don't mind you staying in here."

Leonard turned around. "I'm just going back to my cabin."

Ruth felt a little sad tug. "But Master Leonard! It's been my pleasure to serve you."

Leonard looked at her thoughtfully. "I know," he said finally. "And I thank you for it. But you needn't take care of me anymore, that is all."

Ruth nodded, but inwardly she wished he'd stay around a little longer. She just wanted to make sure he really was going to be alright. But, maybe he was right. Taking care of just herself felt a little overwhelming at the moment, with how tired she was. Leonard turned to walk away.

Ruth limped over to the galley. Sinking into a chair, she rested her head on her hand as she tried to start working on breakfast. She sighed, wishing the lightheadedness would go away. As he passed, Leonard's eyebrows furrowed.

A short while later, Sean walked past the galley on his way to the top deck. He glanced into the galley, then did a double take as he realized Ruth's pose. She looked exhausted.

Concern crossed Sean's face, and as he walked up to the top deck, he kept an eye out for Captain Edward. Sean spotted him talking with Alessio beside the mast. When Alessio finally walked away, Sean raised a hand to get Captain Edward's attention. "Captain."

Captain Edward took a few steps toward Sean. "What is it?"

Sean shuffled over to him before continuing. Captain Edward noticed the slightly serious expression on his face. "What is it?" Captain Edward repeated.

"Captain," Sean said quietly. "The girl's acting sick."

"What do you mean?"

"She looks exhausted," Sean answered, "and I never thought this would strike me as strange, but she's not singing. She's always been singing."

"Hmm." Captain Edward was beginning to look concerned. "I'll check on her."

"Think about it," Sean continued. "She's been taking care of all of us who are sick, even giving up sleep which could *keep* her from getting sick. What are the chances that she's *not* going to catch it?"

Captain Edward's brow furrowed. "I'll check on her," he repeated. His heart sank at the thought of Ruth being sick. It was amazing how quickly the sick men had recovered. God had obviously shown His favor on them. But what if Ruth fell ill now? How serious would it be? Would God heal her favor like He had the others? Surely He would, but there was no way to know what God should choose to do. But before worrying himself like this, Captain Edward just needed to see if Sean was right.

As soon as Captain Edward got the chance, he headed down the stairs to find Ruth. He found her in the galley, slowly arranging cups of water on the table. "How are you this morning, Ruth?" he asked casually.

Ruth heaved a sigh and shrugged. "I'm fine."

Captain Edward noticed how slowly she was moving and her weary voice. "Ruth," he asked, "are you alright?"

Ruth shrugged again, repeating, "I'm fine."

Captain Edward knew better. She wasn't *really* fine. Her face was pale, and it held a frown. Not the kind like when you're angry, but the sort that happens when you're so tired you just don't have the energy to prop up a smile. And her sunny, cheerful voice had faded into a weary mumble hardly louder than a mouse's.

Captain Edward walked over to beside her. Ruth didn't look up from her work. She wasn't quite sure why, but she didn't want the sailors knowing she might be sick. Maybe because she wasn't sure how they treat her if *she* was the one who was weak. Oh, most of the time they didn't bother her anymore, but Ruth's brain was too tired to really sort through the logic of it.

With Captain Edward, however, Ruth felt differently. She trusted him. He'd never laughed at her, made her feel threatened, or acted like she was weird. So once he was beside her, and she felt no one in the hall was watching, she didn't hesitate to look him in the eye and let him see how exhausted she really was.

Captain Edward looked closer at her pale face. Her usually-shining eyes were now gray clouds, pleading to know someone cared. Captain Edward gently felt her forehead and placed the back of his hand to her cheek. Ruth watched him with tired eyes.

"I don't think you've got a fever," Captain Edward decided, taking his hand off her face. "Do you *feel* sick?"

Ruth sighed. "I'm too tired to be able to tell," she said in a small voice.

Captain Edward nodded. "Alright. After breakfast, I want you to get some rest," he said gently.

Ruth sighed, feeling overwhelmed. "But—"

Free

"How about this," Captain Edward smiled playfully, trying to lighten things a bit. "After breakfast, you have *captain's orders* to get some rest."

Ruth couldn't help but smile. "Captain's orders?"

"Captain's orders," Captain Edward smiled back.

"Alright," Ruth agreed. "I will."

"Alright. Good." Captain Edward nodded at her before leaving the room.

As Captain Edward walked down the hall, he began praying. "God, I know You already have a plan, but I just have to ask You. Please don't let Ruth fall ill. She's served You so faithfully. In don't want anything to happen to her. I know no one probably *deserves* mercy, but it seems like Ruth does. I'm sorry if I'm not saying this right, but You know what I mean. Amen."

Captain Edward sighed, feeling a clash of emotions. He felt peace knowing he had trusted God as Ruth's Healer, but at the same time it was hard knowing there wasn't much he could do to protect Ruth from this.

Meanwhile, Ruth sighed and tried to pick up her pace. After a few more minutes, Ruth had breakfast ready and the men were gathering in the galley.

Ruth did her best to act normal as the men ate their breakfast, but try as she might, she couldn't escape Hector's sharp eye. Once breakfast was through and everyone was heading their separate ways, Hector lowered his voice and looked at Captain Edward. "Captain, is she ill?"

Captain Edward stroked his beard. "Well, I'm not sure. I was actually wondering if you might take a look at her for me."

Hector agreed. "I can do that."

Several rooms down the hall, Ruth lay sprawled out on her bed nibbling at her food. This just didn't taste good. Not on a stomach that was bothering her. Not that she thought she was going to be sick, but her stomach just felt yucky. Tears of exhaustion began slowly trickling down her cheeks.

Knock, knock, knock. Someone was at the door. *Great,* Ruth thought mournfully. *Now they're going to see me like this!* She didn't mind if Captain Edward figured out she'd been crying, but she didn't want all the other men to know!

Ruth wiped her face and tried to put on a normal voice. "Who calls?"

Captain Edward's concern grew. Ruth always came to the door. This wasn't like her. He cracked the door a bit so she could hear him. "Ruth, come here a moment. I want Hector to look at you."

Ruth's eyes widened. Yikes! Now someone WAS going to know! But she figured Captain Edward knew what was best for her. Hesitantly, she slid out of bed and to the door.

Captain Edward motioned for her to follow him. "Come. Let's go to the galley." He noticed her red eyes.

Ruth walked beside him until they came to the galley. Peering in, she saw Hector waiting for them. Ruth stopped.

"Come on," Captain Edward urged gently.

Ruth followed him inside. Captain Edward sat on one of the stools, and Ruth sank onto the one beside him.

Hector scooted his seat to in front of her. Ruth tensed up. This was going to be awkward.

First, Hector stood up and felt Ruth's face. His big hands hardly fit on her small forehead. He then sat back down. "Here, let me feel your teeth," he said.

Ruth puckered her brow. "Why? Why would…"

"Just let him," Captain Edward assured her. "He's trying to figure out if you have scurvy."

Ruth didn't know what scurvy was, but knew she didn't want to have it, whatever it was. She obediently opened her mouth.

It was weird to have his huge hand in her mouth, but after he gently pushed on and wiggled a few of her teeth, he was done. "Nope," Hector said to himself. He thought a moment. "Hmm…are you seasick?"

Ruth heaved a sigh. The quick answer was yes, but it wasn't something she wanted to talk about. Just hearing the word *seasick* made her stomach feel worse. Ruth stared at the floor. "I don't want to say," she mumbled sheepishly.

Captain Edward felt a tinge of frustration. How could this girl, so quick to help others she hardly knew, be so stubborn when they tried to help her? Swallowing a sigh, he reminded himself she wasn't feeling well. Putting his arm around her, he rubbed her shoulder. "Come now, Ruth," he whispered. "It's not like you have to tell the whole crew. Are you seasick or not?"

Ruth felt tears welling up in her eyes again. She wanted to be in her room, sleeping right now, not telling someone she didn't know how badly she felt! Ruth admitted, "Yeah. A little."

"Alright," Hector nodded. "…do you feel like you're going to be sick?"

"Oh, no, no," Ruth quickly responded. "Well, at least not at the moment."

"Alright." Hector sat for a moment, contemplating Ruth's symptoms. As he waited for Hector to decide, Captain Edward rubbed Ruth's shoulder.

"Well," Hector began, "For the moment, I don't think she's ill. She doesn't have a fever, and she doesn't appear to have scurvy. I think she's just exhausted from working so hard."

Captain Edward nodded. "Alright. Ruth, you can go get some rest now."

Ruth slowly lifted her head off Captain Edward's shoulder. "Alright. Thank you." Slowly she walked to the door.

"Captain's orders," teased Captain Edward.

Ruth turned around, and for the first time all day, she laughed. "Aye, sir," she returned playfully.

Ruth disappeared down the hall, and Captain Edward chuckled fondly. He had just realized something: for the first time in his life, he had a girl who wanted his support. Not in a romantic way, but in a fatherly way; in the simple sense that she trusted him to protect her, look out for her, take care of her. They had a bond. A mutual respect. A two-way relationship. And that was special.

Captain Edward walked out of the galley and back down the hall to return to his work. By now, a couple of the other men had figured out Ruth's situation. Alessio and Charles walked by, and Charles had to ask. "Captain, is she alright?"

"Hector says she should be fine," Captain Edward answered plainly. He figured Ruth would appreciate him not sharing any details. "Cut her some slack. She's been up late a lot."

Free

Charles sighed. "Surely her God will protect her. She has a relationship with Him." Charles' normally cheerful eyes were now serious as he raised them to Captain Edward's.

Captain Edward's chest tightened. He knew that look. He knew what Charles was feeling, because he had felt it himself. It was the feeling of God tugging on your heart, telling you He wants a relationship with you…but at the same time a feeling of fear because you know you need a relationship with Him, yet you're not ready.

"God is good," Captain Edward assured Charles. "And He does good things…even if they aren't our idea of good. He sees a bigger picture than we do."

"So… is she going to be alright?" wondered Alessio.

Captain Edward shrugged. "I don't know," he sighed. "But God does."

Charles and Alessio exchanged a nervous glance before continuing down the hall. As they went on with their day, Charles' thoughts tossed, and Alessio was beginning to feel a tug. God wanted to be their Friend, just as He was for Ruth and Captain Edward

Charles couldn't get it off his mind. It didn't help matters that his duty was to stand up in the crow's nest all by himself. Being alone only made the voices in his head louder, and he didn't know what to do with them.

When at last it was time for his meal break, Charles climbed down from the lookout. Ruth was still asleep, so the men just made their own meals. After he ate, it was Charles' turn for a break from watch duty. He meandered to the midshipmen's cabin and walked to the corner where his sea chest sat. He sat down in front of it.

Charles unlatched the lock and opened the creaking wooden lid. He began pulling out the trunk's contents: clothes, books, an old spotting scope, and random bits of junk he'd never taken the time to throw away. Soon the floor around Charles was a cluttered mess of his belongings.

As Charles neared the bottom of the chest, he spied the corner of something made of leather. Charles yanked it out. So he *did* still have it! It was his leather-covered Bible.

He flipped open the first page, across which was handwriting. *Charles, always trust God to chart your paths. — Mother.* A smile twitched at Charles' mouth. He could still faintly picture his mother handing him the Bible on the sandy shores of the dock from which he had first set sail years and years ago.

"Charles," his mother had said with teary eyes, "I want you to have this. Never forget the Lord. Follow His ways, and you will have His blessing on your ocean journeys."

Charles had hardly ever read it; maybe even never. But now he felt relieved he still had it. He turned the page. Right there on the floor, with the piles around him, Charles began to read the Word of God.

Chapter Eleven

Winds of Change

Therefore, if anyone is in Christ, *he is* a new creature; the old things passed away; behold, new things have come.

(2 Corinthians 5:17 NASB)

*A*n hour later, Captain Edward was walking down the hall. Charles emerged from the cabin. "Oy, Captain," he called, "Do you have a moment?"

"Of course," Captain Edward agreed. "What is it?"

Charles's face was one big smile. Charles was usually a cheerful person, but this radiant smile was nothing like Captain Edward had ever seen before.

Charles burst out laughing, and Captain Edward was now truly curious. "What? What is it?" he persisted, excitement running in his veins.

"I'm saved now!" Charles declared.

Captain Edward's jaw dropped, and for a moment he was speechless. Recovering from his shock, he quickly put his arm around Charles' shoulders in a hug. "Aye, Charles, that's wonderful!"

Before he could say anything more, an uneven-sounding gait ran up the hall. Ruth had just been waking up, but at overhearing the words "I'm saved now" she was flying out of bed and up the hall. Suddenly, she realized this wasn't her conversation, and in her ecstasy, she'd walked right into it. Ruth hesitated just as she reached the two men.

Charles grinned at the curious, uncertain face. "Aye, lass, you heard, didn't you?"

Ruth grinned sheepishly. "Is it true?" she asked bashfully.

"Aye, mistress. And I know who I ought to thank." There was a twinkle in his eye.

Ruth took a moment to understand what he meant. Then she chuckled and shook her head. "No, no, you don't thank me. You thank God." She pointed at the ceiling.

Charles smiled. "Well, thank you anyway." He turned to walk down the hall, and nearly crashed into Alessio, who, by the look on his face, had just listened to the whole conversation.

Charles pleasantly continued, but Alessio followed. "Charles," he whispered hoarsely, "what was it like?"

Charles turned. He looked thoughtfully at Alessio's uneasy face. "What was what like?"

Alessio's face turned white. "Whatever it is they call it. You know, getting...converted."

"Aye." Charles thought a moment. "It's freeing."

"Freeing?" Alessio looked surprised. "But, Charles, just think of all the rules you'll have to follow. You'll be just like Captain Edward. Your life will be so boring."

Charles' brow furrowed as he considered his friend's honest question. "This freedom is as exciting as anything," he said finally. "Look at the girl. She serves the Lord with heart and soul, and she doesn't act like she's pent up with rules."

Alessio's gaze turned down the hall as he was lost in thought. Charles waited patiently, in case Alessio was going to ask another question; but after a long silence, he continued down the hall.

"Charles," Alessio called after him, though in a subdued voice. "I want it. I want the freedom. It's freedom from death, isn't it?"

"Aye," answered Charles. "And fear of it. And it seems to me, with the way the girl carries herself and now Captain Edward, perhaps it is a kind of help with all fear."

Alessio and Charles then found themselves swallowed in silence, for Charles didn't know how to explain the Gospel to Alessio; nor was either brave enough to go to a young girl over the matter.

Then, Captain Edward walked past. "Oy, captain," blurted Charles, before he realized what he was doing, "Where's the girl?"

Captain Edward gave them a suspicious look, but he sensed Charles' sincerity. "Why?" he asked.

"I…we…Alessio wants to ask her something," Charles stammered.

A few minutes later, Ruth was patiently explaining the Gospel to Alessio, with Charles and Captain Edward standing with him. Alessio hardly waited for her to finish. "Aye, Ruth," he said with joy radiating on his face. "I'm ready. I believe in God. Jesus shall be my Lord. I want the freedom you have, even if I must adhere to rules."

Ruth's heart swelled with joy, and she exchanged a glance with Captain Edward. "It's not about rules," she explained with a smile. "Nothing you could do would earn or take God's love. Rather, doing things that please Him come out of gratefulness for what He has done for you."

Captain Edward smiled and laid his hand on Alessio's shoulder. "Let's pray."

They all knelt side-by-side in the narrow hall. Each one prayed, and as she listened to the men praying to Jesus, Ruth could hardly contain her excitement. Now she was more than a passenger on this ship—she was among a family in Christ.

At the last "Amen", Ruth opened her eyes and threw her arms around Captain Edward's neck. "Praise God, from whom all blessings flow!" she exclaimed. "Now we're a family!" Any bit of exhaustion left in her was now overwhelmed with joy.

Suddenly Alan appeared from a nearby doorway. "What on earth are you doing out here?"

Ruth's face glowed. "We are brothers and sisters in Christ now," she answered, motioning to the sailors beside her.

Alan narrowed his eyes.

"We're serving the Lord together," Ruth explained, standing up.

"So, you guys have some *religious club* now?" Alan didn't seem to know what to make of this.

"It's not a club, Alan," said Charles. "It's a calling."

"And you're welcome to join us," offered Ruth.

"Oh," Alan chuckled nervously. "No, thanks. I'm not ready for that yet." He disappeared back into the room.

Ruth watched him leave, and then sighed happily. "Well, I'd better be getting to my work."

"Alright," Alessio agreed, standing up. "Me too. Thank you for all your help, Ruth."

Ruth beamed. "Give God the glory!" she answered. "I am just his tool." She began down the hall, her lopsided steps light and happy.

As Ruth went to look for a broom, she pondered a wonderful truth. *I'm not alone anymore,* she thought happily. *I mean, I never truly was because I had You, God. But now I have earthly brothers on this ship, too.*

Ruth's heart swelled with joy. Unable to contain it, she burst out singing:

"O for a thousand tongues to sing

My great Redeemer's praise!

The glories of my God and King,

The triumphs of His grace!

"O gracious Master and my God,

Assist me to proclaim;

To spread through all the earth abroad

The honors of Thy Name!"

Ruth couldn't stop singing. As she swept the sterncastle, she switched to *Amazing Grace.* When she mopped the galley, the strains of *Tis So Sweet to Trust in Jesus* fairly floated from her lips. And later, as she finished the pea soup, *Revive Us Again* bounced off the walls.

Charles walked in, sat down, and propped his feet up on the table. "About ready?"

"Yes," Ruth answered cheerfully. "Here's yours." She held out a bowl.

"Thanks," Charles nodded. He put his feet down and set the bowl on the table. Wisps of steam curled up from the soup. "Do you want me to call the others?"

"If you wouldn't mind." Ruth agreed. She continued filling the tin bowls.

Charles walked to the doorway and stepped into the hall. "Sean!" he yelled. "Ruth's got supper ready!"

Sean sounded his whistle, and Ruth giggled. "You sure can yell a lot louder than I can," she said to Charles.

"Well," Charles chuckled. "You've got to yell loud when you're up in a lookout fifty feet above everyone else."

The sailors began gathering in the galley, and Ruth handed out the bowls. She stood in the doorway, and once everyone was seated, Ruth instinctively closed her eyes and folded her hands. But then her eyes popped open. *Oh, that's right,* she thought. *These sailors have probably never prayed before they eat.*

Captain Edward noticed her. "Shall we pray?" he suggested.

Bushy eyebrows raised, but Ruth smiled and nodded. Captain Edward bowed his head and closed his eyes. Ruth, Alessio, and Charles did the same. The other sailors shifted uneasily, exchanging unsure glances.

Charles nudged Jonas. "Your hat."

Jonas looked confused. "What's wrong with it?"

"Take it off."

Jonas still looked confused, but he hesitantly pulled his hat off his head.

Captain Edward was already praying: "God, thank You for this food. Thank You for Ruth and that she could make it for us. Amen."

"Amen," chorused Ruth, Alessio, and Charles. Spoons clinked against bowls as the sailors began eating. Ruth grabbed her bowl. "Captain Edward thanked God for me," she thought with a smile. She stood in the doorway.

Charles turned toward her. "You're welcome to join us, Ruth," he said. "There's a seat over there by Sean."

"Oh," Ruth chuckled nervously. "No, thanks. I'll just stay right here." She didn't mind eating *near* the sailors — as long as they didn't get rowdy — but sitting in the middle of them? She wasn't quite ready for that yet.

Ruth stood in the doorway for a while, sipping at her soup. Towards the end of the meal, the sailors started getting loud and a little wild. Captain Edward glanced up and saw that Ruth had disappeared.

Up the hall, Ruth was walking to her room. She was a little let down, but she was still smiling. *Sometime soon,* she thought, *I'll be able to stay. Sometime soon.*

Careena Campbell

Free

Chapter Twelve

Eternal Fire

"Greater love has no man than this, that one lay down
his life for his friends."

(John 15:13 NASB)

S wishhh…swishhh…swishhh…

Stephan listened to the purr of the waves as he
stood in the crow's nest. The ship rocked gently back
and forth as he scanned the night skies for danger.

As he stood there, he pondered Captain
Edward's changes to their ship life. It all seemed so
strange. He didn't mind if Captain Edward chose not to
stay up late being rowdy, but to make everyone else do
the same? Stephan didn't like it. And praying before
they ate — it just felt awkward. It made him — and
everyone else — realize that Captain Edward's
commitment to God was much more real than they had
thought. He didn't just *say* he was serving God, he was
really doing it. Stephan didn't like the changes at all.
What good were they supposed to do but satisfy one
man's conscience? Then, from some strange, hidden
hollow of his mind, Stephan's own conscience surfaced.
Yet he didn't know what it was saying, so he shoved it
back into its little hiding place in his mind.

Stephan's thoughts were suddenly interrupted
as he caught a whiff of a strange scent. Kind of like
smoke. What would smell like that? No, it wasn't
coming from his lantern. What was it then?

"Oy!" yelled Theodore from the deck. "Do you smell smoke?"

"Aye," Stephan answered, alarm rising in his chest. "Where's it coming from? Surely no one's cooking at this hour!"

"I don't know," Theodore replied. "Do you see anything?"

Stephan alertly scanned his surroundings. In the moonlight, his eyes traced a small black silhouette rising from the stern.

Stephan's heart hammered. "Smoke!" he yelled down. "I see —"

Jonas bolted up the stairs. "FIRE!" he yelled. "THE CARGO HOLD IS ON FIRE!"

Stephan raced down the ladder as Jonas rang the alarm bell. "ALL HANDS ON DECK!" he shouted. "Fire in the stern!"

Theodore was already tearing through the hall below deck. "MEN! GET UP! FIRE! TO THE FIRE!" A hurricane of action ensued as the sailors flung themselves out of bed and began rushing up and down the corridor.

Captain Edward appeared in the hall as smoke began drifting in. Instantly, he was running to join the others.

"Mistress Brett!" Augustus's voice rang out. "Get up! Fire!" He pounded on her door.

A startled Ruth appeared in the doorjamb and Captain Edward quickly explained the situation. "Ruth, there's a fire. Come up to the top deck. We're trying to put it out."

Ruth was already limping up the hall behind him. "What if you can't?" she wondered aloud.

"We'll face it then," Captain Edward returned. "Faster, men," he ordered the sailors, "or we'll be burned to our deaths!"

Sailors brushed past, holding buckets of water. Sloshes of water, smoke, and sailors became a blur as they rushed to extinguish the flames before the ship was doomed.

"What can I do?" Ruth yelled as she stepped foot on the top deck.

"Pray!" Captain Edward called back.

Ruth glanced out over the ocean before bursting into song:

"Eternal Father, strong to save,

Whose arm hath bound the restless wave,

Who bids the mighty ocean deep

Its own appointed limits keep…"

When Captain Edward heard her singing, he momentarily froze. He recognized the song. It was the song that Captain Thomas—the man who had trained him to sail—had taught him many years ago. As Ruth's voice rang out the words, they began coming back to Captain Edward, just as the kind old captain had taught him.

"O hear us when we cry to Thee…" his strong, deep voice blended with Ruth's delicate high one as he began to sing the notes: "…for those in peril on the sea."

The other sailors were surprised to hear Captain Edward singing. Was that a hymn he was singing? He sang their working chants, but never this kind of song.

Still, the prayers continued to rise as the two friends begged for God's mercy:

"O Christ, whose almighty word

The wind and waves, submissive, heard

Who walked upon the foaming deep

And calm amid its rage did sleep:

O hear us when we cry to Thee

For those in peril on the sea!"

Captain Edward's song was broken up as he communicated with the men, but he always joined Ruth for that last refrain: "O hear us when we cry to Thee...for those in peril on the sea."

Above all the chaos, the pleading notes soared higher and higher as if they would fly through past the sails and burst into the clouds.

"Most Holy Spirit, who did brood

Upon the chaos dark and rude,

Who bid its angry tumult cease,

And gave, for wild confusion, peace;

O hear us when we cry to Thee

For those in peril on the sea!"

Back and forth, up and down the sailors rushed, hoping to have some chance of beating the fire.

"What's our status?" Captain Edward yelled.

Stephan's voice called back: "We think it's working, but there's still a lot of smoke, probably from where it was still wet from the leak. I don't think it's touched the ship's body yet, just the cargo. We're trying to figure out if we've put it out or not!"

"Where's Leonard?" yelled somebody.

Ruth gasped, her eyes widening as she listened to the exchange that followed.

Free

"He's in the room that's on fire."

Ruth felt a strange sensation. Her mind flashed with scenes. What if Leonard was stuck, or got hurt? Without really thinking, she followed the strange draw down the stairs.

A few moments later, Captain Edward glanced around. Where was Ruth? He called her name, but there was no answer. Leonard appeared at the top of the stairs. "Oy!" he yelled. "Why's that girl in the hall?" He sounded irritated.

Captain Edward couldn't believe his ears. "What! She knows better than that." Indignant and concerned for her safety, he hurried across the deck and down the steps.

He searched for Ruth, but he didn't see her among the sailors. "Oy!" shouted Stephan. "That girl's lost her wits!"

"Where is she?" Captain Edward shouted.

"She's mad, is where she is! I tried to stop her, but she waltzed right past me into the hold!"

Ruth hadn't seen Leonard when they'd passed in the corridor. The sailors had tried to stop her, but she'd only brushed past them. She stumbled into the smoke-filled cargo hold. "Leonard—" she coughed, but there was no answer. She stepped farther in. "L—" she began, but the air was too thick and hot to breathe. Menacing heat blazed through the air. She stepped in further and was about to call again when she tottered on her short leg and tumbled to the floor. Her heart hammering, she forced herself to her hands and knees. It was too dark to see, and smoke choked her. It dawned on her that Leonard wasn't here, and her short leg was going to make it hard to get out quickly! She heard voices, and she knew the sailors were coming back to put more water on the fire. Now deep in the cargo hold

159

and fighting for breath, Ruth began aimlessly crawling back toward the door. The sailors would find her.

Suddenly, Ruth realized Captain Edward was calling her: "Ruth!" He coughed as he hit the cloud of smoke. "Where are you?"

"Here," Ruth choked feebly from the other side of the room.

Captain Edward stepped carefully into the smoke. "Ruth," he called again as the sailors brushed by him with buckets of water.

"Over here," Ruth repeated, but she was running out of air. Her body unable to go any further, Ruth flopped onto the floor as her thoughts fogged and spun like the smoke.

Captain Edward still wasn't sure where Ruth was relative to where he was standing. "Ruth!" he called into the haze. He waited for an answer, but there was none.

Captain Edward panicked, a sick feeling squeezing into his chest. He pulled his shirt over his nose, got down on his hands and knees, and began desperately feeling around the room.

Heat blazed through the choking smoke. Finally, Captain Edward's fingers brushed what felt like an arm. Panting, he pulled Ruth into his arms and stumbled out of the smoky room. Water splashed under his feet.

Up the stairs he ran as several of the men brushed by. The other sailors stared wide-eyed at the girl lying unconscious in Captain Edward's arms. "What happened?" gasped Charles.

Captain Edward shook his head. "I'm not sure." For a moment, he stood holding Ruth as if unsure of what to do. He then sat her up on a barrel. "Hector! Get over here! And Alan, I want a status report! There was water under my feet in the hold."

The men stood in grave silence as they waited. At last, Alan emerged from below deck and announced, "The fire's out!"

Sighs of relief and a few cheers erupted from the sailors.

"But what about the water?" Captain Edward objected. "Where did it come from?"

"Well, you're not going to believe it," Alan answered, flashing a huge grin at Sean, "but the leak came unplugged just long enough to finish putting out the fire! We got to it before it caused damage in itself, but it actually saved the ship!"

"WHAT!" Captain Edward gasped in astonishment. "God be praised. He spared our lives."

Sean walked up and looked down at Ruth's closed eyes and still figure. Hector knelt beside her, trying to revive her. Concern lay in Sean's eyes as he raised them to Captain Edward's. "Is she alright?"

Captain Edward shook his head. "I don't know." He knelt next to Ruth, still holding up her shoulders. "Hector —"

Suddenly, Ruth coughed feebly. Her eyes fluttered open, slowly focusing on her surroundings.

"Oh, thank You, Lord," Captain Edward breathed.

Ruth's foggy thoughts slowly cleared, her weary face pale as she tried to remember what had just happened.

"Are you alright?" Captain Edward asked anxiously.

Ruth coughed before answering. "I think so," she whispered.

Evident relief flooded over Captain Edward, and a smile pulled at his lips as he rubbed her shoulder.

Stephan walked up. "What on earth were you doing?" he demanded. His voice sounded astonished, indignant, and confused.

Ruth looked up. She tried to make sense of the strange urge she had felt to go in and help Leonard, when he hadn't even ended up being in there. "I thought Leonard was trapped in there," she finally answered.

"But he wasn't," Theodore objected.

"But I just wanted to make sure," Ruth answered.

"Foolishness," scoffed Ronan. "Don't you know you could've suffocated in there?"

Ruth shrugged. "I'd rather risk my life in a fire so someone else can get another chance to accept salvation than do nothing and know an unbeliever might die. If an unbeliever dies, he's going to hell — and there, it's eternal fire!" Passion dripped off Ruth's words.

First Mate Leonard's gaze was fixed to the floor. "That's all fine, but I don't deserve your mercy."

Ruth smiled. "No one does, but God gave it to me anyway. I wanted to be a picture of the mercy He gave me."

Silent awe stole over the ship. The passion in Ruth's words seemed to echo across the deck, touching every ear. "But why did *you* need that mercy?" Augustus questioned. "You're as decent of a lass as exists."

Ruth smiled, glancing around in amazement. All the sailors' eyes were on her. Their questions could be answered with the Gospel.

Ruth's heart beat fast. This was a moment she had waited for her whole life.

"Arise, shine, for your light has come,
And the glory of the LORD has risen upon you.
Lift up your eyes round about and see;
They all gather together, they come to you…"
(Isaiah 60:1,4 NASB)

Careena Campbell

Chapter Thirteen

Ransomed

There is neither Jew nor Greek, there is neither slave nor free man, there is neither male nor female; for you are all one in Christ Jesus.

(Galatians 3:28 NASB)

*R*uth said a quick prayer before answering. "Well," she began, "I've done wrong things, just like anyone else. And since God is just, he hates sin, and He has to punish sin. His punishment for sins — no matter how small they seem — is death and eternal separation from Him. But God sent His Son, Jesus, to the earth. Jesus was fully God, so He never sinned. But He took the death penalty anyway to pay for *our* sins. The Bible says in Isaiah, 'But he *was* wounded for our transgressions, *he was* bruised for our iniquities: the chastisement of our peace *was* upon him; and with his stripes we are healed.'

"Jesus died on a cross. In the Bible it says, 'Greater love hath no man than this, that a man down his life for his friends.' But," Ruth interjected, her face radiant, "Jesus didn't stay dead. Three days later, God miraculously raised Him from the dead! Now He sits at God's right hand.

"By placing your faith in Jesus, you are accepting God's free gift of salvation through Jesus' death. You will still die on this earth, but you will be spared from the 'second death,' which is eternal separation from God in hell. While you're on the earth, the Holy Spirit will help be your guide. And in the life to come, you will live in heaven with God."

"So," said Jonas, "You were just trying to follow Jesus' example, weren't you?"

"Yes!"

"Why?"

Ruth's face glowed. "When God has done something so amazing for you, you want to serve Him any way you can find! And one way to do that is to imitate His example."

The sailors listened intently in amazement. They had all gathered around Ruth— except for Leonard, who stood a short distance away. Charles, Alessio, and Captain Edward waited quietly, hoping their fellow sailors might be about to get saved.

A long pause reigned as the men considered what Ruth had said. They realized what she was saying could have an implication on their very lives. Suddenly, what she had done had called them to a choice of their own. Finally, Augustus asked, "Does following God make life easy?"

"Well, not exactly," Ruth said with a slight laugh. "Life on this earth certainly hasn't been easy for me. But knowing God is with you, watching you, and going to reward you for faithfulness helps to get you through the rough times. To some, I may be a slave. But I'm not a slave to sin. Salvation has set me free, and no man can enslave me again."

"But I'm a mess," objected Stephan. "I've hung out with the wrong people in the wrong ways. I'm not good enough."

Captain Edward chuckled to himself. "I know *that* feeling. But I was just reading in the Bible about a man named Saul. He hated the Christians and even had some of them killed. And then Jesus appeared to him. Saul became a Christian missionary. If Jesus wants a murderer to become His child, I think He wants anyone."

Alan nodded, and silence reigned again. Seconds hung as if they had been hours. No words were spoken. The sailors all seemed deep in thought. Ruth and Captain Edward stood motionless, praying earnestly for them to make the decision. They glanced over to Charles and Alessio, who appeared to be doing the same. All was still and calm.

After a long pause, some of the men began to go their separate ways. Eventually, only Charles and Alessio were standing near Ruth and Captain Edward. Ruth's heart sank a little, but the flicker of hope within her was still alive. They might not be ready to accept salvation now, but they very well might be soon.

After making certain Ruth was now alright, Captain Edward got up. Charles and Alessio followed him. They went below deck, probably to evaluate the fire damage. Ruth sat, alone, on the barrel. She didn't want to go to bed yet. She just couldn't. She had a feeling these men were closer to accepting salvation then it seemed. Ruth stood up and limped to the edge of the ship. She closed her eyes, folded her hands, and prayed.

It wasn't more than ten minutes later that Theodore walked up from below deck. "Ruth," he said.

Ruth whipped around.

"I can't stand it anymore," Theodore sighed. "I'm ready. How can I be saved?"

Before Ruth could even answer, Sean walked up. "Me too."

Ruth glanced around. She drew in her breath as she realized the others were coming back, one by one, standing nearby, watching. Everyone wanted to know — well, everyone except for Leonard. He was standing far away on the forecastle. This was Ruth's moment—or rather, God's moment to use her to lead some new sons through the gate of His Kingdom.

For a moment, Ruth didn't know what to say. She silently prayed for wisdom, then turned to see Captain Edward flipping open his Bible with a huge smile on his face. While he had been below deck, he had slipped it in his pocket just in case this really did happen. And now it was happening! He flipped to Romans and read the same verse Ruth had read to him: "'That if thou shalt confess with thy mouth the Lord Jesus, and shalt believe in thine heart that God hath raised him from the dead, thou shalt be saved.'"

While waiting for a response, Ruth glanced up to see where Leonard was. He was nowhere in sight. Ruth said a quick prayer for Leonard and then turned back to the situation at hand. She made eye contact with each of the men as she asked them: "Do you believe God raised Jesus from the dead?"

Heads nodded as voices chorused, "Yes."

Ruth's smile grew bigger, and her heart raced with anticipation. She glanced at Captain Edward, who was just as excited. "Now," Ruth declared, "it's time to confess Jesus as Lord."

"How do we do that?" asked Augustus, a smile turning up on his face.

"Well, you could pray, stand up and say it, or both!"

"I'll go for both!" declared Alan, with his signature decided tone. "Lord Jesus, You are Lord of all, and I promise to serve You forever!"

"Amen!" echoed Stephan, standing up. "Jesus will be my Lord from now on!"

Free

Sean's hearty voice carried across the deck: "No matter what happens, I will serve the Lord Jesus!"

Across the deck, the rest of the sailors echoed, some raising their hands, others staring reverently into the starry sky.

Ruth clapped her hands together. "Praise the Lord!" she rejoiced. "Now we are one big family!" Charles and Alessio cheered from the lookouts. Captain Edward threw his arms around each of the men's shoulders, and they all laughed together, rejoicing in these men's salvation.

As the laughter died down, Hector suggested they pray. They formed a circle with their hands on each other's shoulder and bowed their heads.

Each man prayed, thanking God for His gift, helping them to accept that gift, and the example Ruth had been of that gift. As she listened to the men praying, Ruth heart swelled with joy.

This is the fulfillment of it all, she thought. *All those hard days, all those tears I cried...I had no idea it would lead to THIS! Thank You SO much, God, for helping me persevere and be Your tool to bring these men to You! Bless them, Lord, as much as You've blessed me.*

The moment was so peaceful, as if at any moment they would be caught up to heaven. After the last man prayed, everyone chorused, "Amen!"

Laughs and shouts of joy rose up again in the victorious celebration of salvation. "This is amazing!" Sean exclaimed. "Such freedom, such a burden has been lifted that—"

"LAND HO!" First Mate Leonard's voice blew from the bow.

The others gasped. Captain Edward ran to the bow and looked where Leonard was pointing. His jaw dropped.

Ruth and the others peered around the mast. There, on the horizon, was the outline of land!

"HUZZAH!" Ruth yelled, clapping her hands. Her heart felt like it would fly right out of her chest with joy. "It only gets better!"

"Where are we?" Captain Edward asked Leonard.

"I'm not sure," Leonard shrugged with amazement. "But, I mean, the fact is we came to land, how — we thought we were miles away, in the heart of the bay!" His voice conveyed his astonishment.

Ruth proclaimed, "We serve a great God! That's how!" She turned back toward the other sailors. "You all want to sing a song?"

"Uh —" Leonard interjected, "we, uh, need to pull the ship in."

"We can sing while we work," assured Alan.

"Do you guys know Amazing Grace?" Ruth suggested. "It was written by a sailor."

"Not really," answered Captain Edward, "but I think I heard you singing it the other day. Go ahead and sing it a couple of times. We'll join in where we can."

Augustus went to the rudder. Charles and Alessio climbed to the lookouts. Sean directed the men as they trimmed the sails while First Mate Leonard and Captain Edward oversaw the process. Ruth marched to the very front of the bow and placed one of her foot on top of a small crate. The rocking of the ship didn't make her wobble a bit anymore.

Free

The sun was just about to come up, its soft yellow light glowing along the horizon. A refreshing breeze blew, sweeping Ruth's hair off her face. With a deep breath, she hoped to express all that she was feeling. Her immense joy came bubbling up from her heart and pouring over her lips in triumphant melody:

"Amazing grace! How sweet the sound!

That saved a wretch like me!

I once was lost, but now I'm found,

Was blind, but now I see!"

"They all gather together, they come to you...

"Then you will see and be radiant,

And your heart will thrill and rejoice;

Because the abundance of the sea will be turned to you.

"Surely the coastlands will wait for Me [the Lord]

And the ships of Tarshish will come first."

(Isaiah 60:4b-5, 9a NASB)

Careena Campbell

Free

Chapter Fourteen

Maybe She Will

*O*nce the ship had docked, Captain Edward and the others began figuring out exactly where they had landed. Turns out they were in a southern French village, at the bottom of the Bay of Biscay. With the help of Gianluca, their interpreter, they traded with the villagers, and then Augustus began planning their return home.

Captain Edward took a break so he could talk to Ruth. Not seeing her on the top deck, he went to see if she was in her room or the galley.

Ruth, meanwhile, was sitting on her bed with her elbows on her knees and her chin resting on her hands. She was deep in thought. Life on this ship was so different now. Even in the few hours that had elapsed since the sailors got converted, things had changed. As they were pulling the ship in, it had seemed to Ruth that the sailors had stayed more patient. Everything seemed to be changing...in a really good way. Suddenly Ruth didn't feel like a stranger or a slave anymore. She was just a passenger...and perhaps even a friend. She was no longer alone. Ruth felt a sad tug at her heart. How many years had she prayed to not be alone!

Suddenly a knock at the door interrupted Ruth's thoughts. She stood up and opened the door. "Yes?"

"Can you come here for a moment?" Captain Edward motioned for her to join him in the hall.

"Of course." Ruth slipped out the door, letting it shut behind her.

Captain Edward took a deep breath before saying, "Well, after we finish here, we're going back to the place we picked you up from. And when we get there..." his voice trailed off. But then, with a nod, he smiled. "I'll let you go back to your parents."

Ruth froze. The sad tug in her heart melted into a flood of emotion. She needed to tell him. As much as she avoided talking about it, it was time to let him know. She sighed deeply, ready to explain, but all that came out was, "I wish you could."

"I can," Captain Edward said in a joking voice. "Leonard won't stop me this time."

Ruth shook her head sadly. "No, no, you don't understand. They're gone. I don't *have* them anymore, Captain Edward."

Captain Edward stopped, surprised. His heart sank as he realized what she was saying. "You mean they're...?"

Ruth shook her head, trying to hold back the tears as memories flashed through her mind. "You've probably figured out that my parents were missionaries." Her voice began to tremble. "My papa was a pastor, although not all of his beliefs lined up with the Church of England. Two years ago, when I was fifteen, my parents felt called to go to Spain..." her voice trailed off. "And you know how dangerous it is for Protestants there."

Captain Edward shuddered. He had heard the horror stories of the Spanish Inquisition, a 150-year-old episode of persecution targeting those who opposed the Roman Catholic church. Protestants had been tortured for their faith. Quietly, he listened as Ruth continued: "We lived in Cádiz for awhile, but my parents wanted to go inland. They left me with a trusted Protestant friend and went just the two of them. They were going to come back and get me, once they had established a place to stay. But…" Ruth's lips quivered as she looked up at Captain Edward. "Three months passed, and they never did come back. They must have been killed, or they would've come back!" A tear slipped onto Ruth's face as her story tumbled out.

Captain Edward could hardly believe what he was hearing. Such a tragic past for such a wonderful young lady. Judging from her strong character, her radiant smile, and her kind loyalty, he never would have guessed she had been through such terrible grief and heartache. Watching Ruth cry, Captain Edward felt like a part of him was missing something too. "Who do you live with, then?"

"Well, I lived with a friend of ours for month or so. But then we got found out and received a summoning to the Inquisition. They arranged for us to sail back to England. Somehow we got separated, and the captain of the ship got confused. He didn't speak very good English, and I think he was expecting an *older* girl, like around eighteen, not a fifteen-year-old who looked like she was twelve. He must've thought it was supposed to be someone else. So he didn't let me board. I missed my ride home!" She swiped her eyes, and her shoulders began to quake.

Captain Edward still didn't understand. "Why hasn't anyone taken you in?" he wondered in amazement.

"Well, a few people have helped me. But it's just so hard to know who to trust. I've been stranded in Spain, remember, and I don't speak the language as well as they do. So I've just had to trust God as my Father and Provider."

"But how have you survived?" Captain Edward knew it was difficult for any homeless orphan to get by, not to mention a girl away from home with a short leg.

"I've learned," Ruth answered. "For the last little while, I've stayed on the edge of town where there are some abandoned buildings. I eat fruit off the trees on the beach. From time to time someone will give me something, and on occasion I've actually had to ask for food. So, a few people are willing to help, but not everybody. I just have to trust God because I'm all alone!" At this point, despite her efforts, Ruth burst out crying. It was loud enough that Charles and Jonas came to see what the trouble was. Captain Edward waved them off. Ruth didn't need anyone staring at her right now.

Charles and Jonas left, and Captain Edward pulled Ruth's head to his chest and wrapped his arm around her shaking shoulders. "There now," he said softly. "You'll be alright. God has always been with you, and He always will be."

Ruth sniffled and took a quivering deep breath. "I know. Most of the time I try to focus on other, more positive things. But sometimes I can't help it. The loneliness is too much."

"Of course." Captain Edward listened quietly, trying to think of something he could say to help Ruth feel better. "You have God," he said softly, "and you have..." he paused. He wanted to say, "you have me," but, well, she wouldn't have him much longer—after she left and all. So he just rubbed her shoulders.

Ruth closed her eyes and let the tears fall. Standing there in Captain Edward's arms felt warm and safe and comforting. It was almost like being in her papa's arms again. The thought sent another tear slipping down her cheek, but at the same time it helped to calm her trembling.

Captain Edward stood quietly, patiently waiting for Ruth to settle down. Sensing she was calming, he decided to get her mind on something else. "Come," he said, letting go of Ruth. "Why don't you race me up the stairs?"

Ruth, glad for the change of subject, dried her eyes. She looked over at the stairway. It sounded like fun, but it also sounded a little silly. "I don't know," Ruth objected sheepishly. "I'm slow. Remember? I have a short leg."

"You've gotten pretty good at it," Captain Edward persisted. "I'll even give you a head start. Come on."

"Alright," Ruth finally agreed, taking her place near the stairs. She felt a rush of adrenaline as Captain Edward's voice called from down the hall: "Ready...set...GO!"

Ruth lunged forward, quickly and carefully scaling the steps. Not more than a few seconds later, Captain Edward came racing up from behind her. His heavy footsteps pounded the floor. Laughing, they placed foot on the top deck at almost exactly the same time.

"You still won!" Ruth giggled.

"Not by much," Captain Edward puffed. "I bet you'll beat me eventually."

Ruth glanced around as she took a moment to catch her breath, squinting in the brilliant sunshine. Sean walked by, carrying a rope over his shoulder and whistling cheerfully. Sitting beside the main mast, Stephan hummed while he worked on mending a sail. Now and then Ruth would recognize a bar of *Amazing Grace*. Of course, if that's what he was humming, he wasn't getting it quite right; but Ruth didn't care. She went to the galley, got the things she needed to wash the dishes, and headed back up to the top deck. She sang along with Stephan's humming as she sloshed dishes and rag in the bucket of cool water.

A short while later, Captain Edward waved to get Alan's and Gianluca's attention. "Oy," he said, "can you come help me see about trading some of this cargo?"

Ruth jumped up. "Can I go?"

Captain Edward looked at her. "Well, I'm not sure there will be much for you to do, but if you want to come, you're welcome to."

"Alright!" Ruth exclaimed, picking up the bucket and walking toward the steps. "I'll be right back!" Ruth didn't care if she couldn't do anything; she could still watch and learn. And really, she just wanted to be with Captain Edward.

A minute later, Captain Edward, Alan, Gianluca, and Ruth were walking down the beach to the merchant posts. Ruth watched quietly as Captain Edward and Alan discussed the trades while Gianluca interpreted. Ruth couldn't understand what the merchants were saying, but based on their curious expressions and what Gianluca claimed they said, they seemed interested. Finally, Captain Edward told Gianluca to tell the men to begin unloading the cargo. Ruth decided she must have been right.

Ruth watched Gianluca return to the ship, then turned to Captain Edward. "What can I do?"

Captain Edward thought for a moment. "I'm not sure, dear." Instantly, his face turned a shade of red as he realized he'd just called Ruth by a nickname. He shook his head with an embarrassed smile.

Ruth, however, didn't find it so strange — she thought it was great! A smile filled her face. Shining with happiness, she limped up the ship's ramp to find something she could do.

Alan grinned as he watched her go. "You just made her day," he mused to Captain Edward. "Man, you've finally got a girl in your life."

Captain Edward turned a little redder, and he looked at Alan incredulously. "Alan, I'm almost forty and she's a teenager."

"No, not that kind of 'girl'," Alan clarified. "Like…a *little* girl. A daughter."

Captain Edward shrugged, but inwardly he had to admit it was true. "She's not ours to keep," he stated modestly.

By now, the other sailors were walking by with barrels and crates. "Let's face it," Alan grinned. "We're all hoping she'll stick around." Lowering his voice, he added, "It's not like she's made any mention of a family. They must not pay much attention to her to let her end up on a ship."

Behind him, Charles set down a barrel. "That doesn't mean she doesn't have one, Alan," he objected.

Alan sighed, but Captain Edward grimaced. "No…no she doesn't."

Alan and Charles looked at him, and so did a couple of the other sailors. Hector looked confused. "She doesn't?"

Captain Edward shook his head. "No. She's an orphan."

"What?" Charles breathed.

"Well, in that case," decided Alan, "she's got to stay! We can look after her."

Captain Edward shook his head again. "It's not our right to keep her here, just as it was not our right to have her here to begin with. The choice is up to her." Looking around at his fellow sailors, he decided, "Under

179

my orders, no one is to push her to stay. If she says she doesn't feel welcome, that's one thing; but I don't want her forced into staying."

The other sailors looked at him a bit sadly. From the beginning, it had never been clear if Ruth would be allowed to leave. As they had gotten to know her better, many had just assumed she'd stay, or at least hang around the ship at the dock. It seemed she was happy here, and that there wasn't anywhere else she needed to be; and honestly, they couldn't imagine life without her now. They had grown to appreciate her cheerful spirit, enjoyed listening to her joyful singing, and really just cared about her. Not in the same way Captain Edward did, but they still wanted her to be somewhere they knew she'd be protected and provided for. Since she was an orphan, if she left, there would be no one except God Himself to do that for her. But Captain Edward was right. The choice was up to her.

Still, they didn't want to accept the possibility of letting go of a girl who really did need them. So as they went back to hauling barrels in and out of the ship, several of the sailors tried to put the thought out of their minds.

Alan looked at Captain Edward. "But—" he began in his usual argumentative sense, but then he stopped himself. "Aye, sir. Whatever you say goes." With that, Alan returned to his work. A surprised smile tugged at Captain Edward's face.

Ruth was down in the galley, wiping off the table. Alan walked in, holding a small crate of vegetables.

"Huzzah!" exclaimed Ruth. "I finally get some new stuff to work with!"

Alan flashed her a smile as he set the crate down and walked back out. Ruth sat down next to the crate

Free

and looked through its contents, contemplating the things she could now make. After all, on this ship, this was a duty reserved for *her*, and she took pleasure in it.

About an hour later, the cargo was stowed and the ship secured. Ruth came up to the top deck to watch the action as the ship got underway.

Many of the men were up in the sails, adjusting and readjusting them as Sean gave them instructions. Charles and Alessio were up in the lookouts, glancing around to get an idea of if there were any unseen sandbars or rocks that the ship might hit as it pulled from the harbor. Several men stood by the ship's port side, lifting the anchor.

"Anchor's aweigh!" they called.

"Aye, aye," responded Sean, then turned to the men in the sails. "Unfurl!" he called.

The sails unfolded, and the wind filled them as the ship began to slowly ease out from the dock. Ruth's heart burst with a sense of adventure. The ship was underway!

She wanted to sing, but she momentarily couldn't think of the right song. Suddenly her ears caught the whisper of a low chant coming from around her. The chant got louder, and Ruth could make out the words: "Ho, we're outward bound. Ho, we're outward bound…"

Ruth realized the sailors were chanting it! Her face lit up. She listened closely as it got louder and louder. She was just about to join in when Alan's voice rang out from up in the sails:

"Man the oar, turn tiller more,

Lest we should run aground.

Leave the shore and raise the board,

181

For, ho! We're outward bound!"

His voice soared through the sails and down to the deck as the other sailors continued to chant in the background. Ruth's face glowed with excitement. Why hadn't she ever heard these sailors singing if they could do it so well? She joined in with the others as they chanted "Ho, we're outward bound" over and over.

Only a few moments after Alan finished singing, Augustus and Sean continued the verse:

"Lookout, do your duty well

And watch for waters rough.

Sail keeper, now man the yard

Don't let the sails be luff."

"Ho, we're outward bound" continued to rise as the anchor detail began the last verse:

"Sailing master, chart our ways

Unto some distant beach…"

The men in the sails finished the song:

"Weigh the anchor, lest it drop

Until the shore we reach."

The chanting got quieter and quieter, and as Jonas walked by carrying a rope, Ruth asked, "How come you all never told me you knew how to sing?"

Jonas smiled and shrugged. "You never asked."

"Ruth," said Augustus, "now that we're Christians, you should write a Christian verse for that song."

Free

"That's a great idea!" Ruth exclaimed. She walked to the edge of the ship. She then burst into song, her heart still chanting with the rhythm:

"God of grace and ocean waves,

Your blessing now bestow.

Guard our ways, and guide our days,

And watch us here below."

Stephan looked impressed. "Oy, that's pretty good."

"Thanks," Ruth grinned.

Across the deck, Theodore nudged Augustus. "She's making up new verses to our chant," he whispered. "Maybe she'll stay."

That night, at supper, Ruth listened quietly as Captain Edward blessed the food. At "Amen", she stood silently in the door, waiting for an invitation.

Hector turned to her. "Please, join us," he offered.

"There's a chair over there by Edward," Alan said, pointing.

Ruth suppressed a smile and slipped over to the spot. Timidly, she sat between Captain Edward and Sean.

She flashed a smile at Captain Edward, but then she heard someone clearing his throat behind her. Her head whipped around. There was First Mate Leonard towering over her. This time, though, it looked like he might actually be amused versus annoyed.

"That's my spot, mistress," he stated with what looked like a hint of a smile.

"Oh," Ruth stammered, feeling a tinge of embarrassment. She quickly bounced out of the chair. "There you go."

Leonard sat down, and several of the men glanced at him incredulously. They were trying to make Ruth feel welcome, and he was concerned about sitting in the proper order?

Ruth, feeling like everyone must be staring at her now, slid past the chairs and out of the room. Captain Edward sighed and looked disapprovingly at Leonard. Leonard wasn't quite sure why this was such a big deal. He knew they were inviting her to be with them, but so what if he still wanted to sit according to his rank?

A few moments later, Ruth slipped back in to grab her bowl.

Captain Edward raised a finger. "Ruth." Glancing around, he spotted a stool along the back wall. Motioning for Alan and Hector to scoot their chairs further down the table, he reached over and slid the stool beside his chair. "Come sit with us," he invited, tapping his hand on the stool.

This time, Ruth couldn't resist smiling. Shyly, she squeezed behind the others' chairs and slipped onto the stool. She smiled at Captain Edward, who smiled back.

Ruth laughed along with the other sailors as the men talked about their various sailing experiences. She was one of the last finished eating, because she was so intently listening in fascination as they told tales of raging seas and wild adventures.

When supper was finished and the dishes cleared, Alan picked up his dusty playing cards off the floor and began shuffling them. "I think I've come to agree with Edward," he remarked. "Not betting is better."

Stephan chuckled. "Aye. I know what you mean. So, what are the teams?"

Alan shrugged. "Eh. It don't matter."

Ruth looked a bit sheepish. She glanced up at Captain Edward in a silent request. Captain Edward caught her glance and smiled. "Alright," he decided. "It'll be Alan, Alessio, Leonard, Sean, and Jonas; then it'll be Charles, Hector, Stephan, Augustus, and Ruth and me."

Ruth's face glowed. As Alan swept cards to each player, Captain Edward explained the game to Ruth. Ruth's eyes sparkled with excitement. She sat up straight on her little stool and picked up the cards she'd been dealt. She tried to arrange them in her hand, but more than once a card fell out onto the table.

"My tiny hands can't hold them all," Ruth remarked nervously. She'd never played card games before.

"You're doing good," Captain Edward approved, observing the cards in her hand. He put his arm around her chair as the men began laying cards into the center of the table.

Within a few moments, it was Ruth's turn. "So…" she said, examining the cards both on the table and in her hand. "Should I play this one?"

Captain Edward set down his cards and looked at Ruth's. "Actually, I would play this one because — " he whispered the reason to her.

"Oh, I get it," Ruth nodded. She picked up the card and whisked it onto the table.

The game lasted awhile as Ruth and the sailors laughed and played together. Captain Edward helped Ruth play her cards, and Ruth returned his kindness as she added her laughter and encouraging spirit to the game.

Eventually the game ended. "It's not too late yet," said Augustus. "We should play again."

Ruth yawned. "It feels pretty late to me."

"You can go to bed if you want," offered Captain Edward.

Ruth shook her head, trying to end the enormous yawn. "I'll stay up for a few more minutes," she said finally.

Alan expertly shuffled the cards. "How about that game we played last week?" he suggested.

Captain Edward looked down at Ruth. "Do you want to learn a new game?" he asked.

Ruth yawned again and laid her head against the back of her chair. "I'll watch," she mumbled sleepily.

Captain Edward put his arm back around her. Sean, who was sitting two seats down from Edward, whispered just loudly enough for him to hear: "Maybe she'll stay."

Captain Edward just shrugged and smiled.

Alan began dealing the cards, and the game began. A few minutes later, Captain Edward felt Ruth's shoulders relax. He glanced down to see Ruth fast asleep. Captain Edward smiled fondly and gently stroked her shoulder. *Maybe she will,* he thought to himself. *Maybe she will.*

Chapter Fifteen

Set Free

*T*he days passed one very much like the others. During the day, Ruth sang along with the believing sailors as they did their respective chores; and in the evening, everyone laughed and talked and played cards together. More than once, Ruth fell asleep leaning on Captain Edward's shoulder.

When Sunday rolled around, Ruth and the other sailors—well, except for First Mate Leonard—laid aside their extra chores and rested whenever they got the chance. Early in the day, Captain Edward asked Ruth if her family ever did anything special on Sundays.

"We had church with other believers," answered Ruth. "We'd read a Scripture passage, sing songs, and pray."

So they did just that.

Ruth and the sailors sat in a group near Augustus, who had to man the rudder. All except Leonard, who didn't want to participate and offered to man the lookout.

Captain Edward and Charles flipped open their Bibles, which all the believers now shared. Ruth wished she could ask First Mate Leonard for hers, but he was already in the lookout. "Does anyone have a suggestion as to where we read?" asked Captain Edward.

Everyone thought for a moment. Finally, Hector said, "Well, I've been reading in John about Jesus' life. I particularly enjoy reading Jesus' speeches to His followers. Let's do that."

"Alright," Captain Edward agreed. It took him a minute to find John, but he got there.

"There," said Hector, pointing to chapter eight. "Start in verse thirty-one. I like that part."

"Alright," Captain Edward nodded. He read verses thirty-one through thirty-three. "'Then said Jesus to those Jews which believed on him, If ye continue in my word, *then* are ye my disciples indeed; And ye shall know the truth, and the truth will make you free. They answered him, We be Abraham's seed, and were never in bondage to any man: how sayest thou, Ye shall be made free?'"

Captain Edward smiled at Ruth as he passed the Bible to Hector. Ruth understood what he meant. These verses spoke of what he'd experienced: the freedom in your heart that comes from standing on the truth of Christ's words.

Hector read the next section. "'Jesus answered them, Verily, verily, I say unto you, Whosoever committeth sin is the servant of sin. And the servant abideth not in the house for ever: *but* the Son abideth for ever. If the Son therefore shall make you free, ye shall be free indeed.'"

As Hector passed the Bible to Alessio, Augustus looked at Ruth. "So that must be where you got that thing you said about not being enslaved to sin."

"Verses like that, yes," Ruth agreed. "I love the picture that paints. Chains of sins, falling off your wrists and vanishing; never to be locked on you again."

The Bible was passed in a circle as each person read a few verses. When at last it returned to Captain Edward, he suggested, "Let's sing *Amazing Grace* now."

Ruth's eyes sparkled. How she loved singing praises to the Lord! "Which verses?" she asked.

Free

"The first two," Captain Edward replied. "I've almost got the first one down, and I'm picking up the second."

Ruth began singing, and the rest joined in where they knew the words:

"Amazing Grace, how sweet the sound

That saved a wretch like me...

"'Twas grace that taught my heart to fear

And grace my fears relieved!

How precious did that grace appear

The hour I first believed!"

Ruth smiled as she sung the words. *Yes,* she thought. *God's grace helped me learn to not be afraid about what others "might" do or what "might"happen. They don't have to tell me I'm "set free". God has set me free already.*

After the song, Captain Edward prayed: "Dear Jesus, thank You for setting us free. Remind us, even when we feel trapped by something, that You are in control and on our side. Amen."

Ruth's heart warmed with joy and peace. That was so true. She really was free.

That night, after supper, the men were bored of playing cards, so they went their separate ways. Ruth walked up to the top deck. The waves gently swept back and forth with their rhythmic hushing, sighing, and blowing on the breeze. The stars overhead smiled and twinkled at Ruth, reflecting in her shining eyes. She took a few steps over to the edge of the ship and stared out over the vast scenery. Her heart filled with the same peace and awe she had felt so many days before, standing near this same spot. It seemed only fitting to sing the same song again:

> "This is my Father's world,
>
> and to my list'ning ears,
>
> All nature sings and round me rings
>
> The music of the spheres.
>
> "This is my Father's world!
>
> I rest me in the thought
>
> Of rocks and trees, of skies and seas
>
> His hand the wonders wrought..."

Ruth heard footsteps behind her, and she looked up to see Captain Edward's smiling face. Ruth smiled back, and as she sang the next verse, Captain Edward hummed along.

> "This is my Father's world,
>
> the birds their carols raise.
>
> The morning light, the lily white
>
> Declare their Maker's praise.
>
> "This is my Father's world!
>
> He shines in all that's fair.
>
> In the rustling grass I hear Him pass,
>
> He speaks to me everywhere."

As she breathed out the final verse, Ruth thought of all that had changed between now and when she had last sung it.

> "This is my Father's world;
>
> O let me ne'er forget
>
> That though the wrong seems oft so strong,

Free

God is the Ruler yet.

"This is my Father's world!

The battle is not done!

Jesus who died shall be satisfied,

The earth and heav'n be one."

So, so much had changed. God had brought her safely to the other side. Yes, she would still have challenges in her life, but He had proven once more that He could see her through them. She had come as a slave, but now was among brothers in Christ—and too, God had shown her what it really means to be free. As she watched the beautiful scenery with Captain Edward by her side, Ruth's heart spun circles of joy and contentment. It felt so good to be free.

Careena Campbell

Chapter Sixteen

Home At Last

"Whereas you have been forsaken and hated with no on passing through, I will make you an everlasting pride, a joy from generation to generation."

(Isaiah 60:15 NASB)

*T*he morning sun dawned bright and cheerful, but the day felt gloomy to many of the sailors. Today the ship was docked in Spain, and today Ruth would leave.

Ruth walked through the corridors looking for First Mate Leonard. She wanted to ask for her Bible before she left. Glancing into one of the cabins, she noticed him sitting on his bed. He had her Bible open.

Ruth wasn't sure Leonard even knew she was there, but if he really *was* reading her Bible, she didn't want to interrupt him. Her eyes sparkled as she walked away. "Oh, Lord," her heart cried, "please help Leonard get saved!"

The men were soon working on loading and unloading cargo. Ruth watched quietly nearby, leaning on the ship's railing. As he passed by, Stephan flashed a smile at Ruth; but Ruth sensed he didn't really feel like smiling.

Ruth, ready to leave, still needed to ask Leonard for her Bible. She turned around and saw him carrying a barrel, with her Bible sitting on top of it. Seeing Ruth, he set the barrel down and silently handed her the Bible.

"Thank you," Ruth said with a smile and a nod.

Leonard nodded back, but he didn't say a word as he picked up the barrel and went back to work.

Ruth glanced around. Looking at Captain Edward, who was overseeing the men, she said, "I'm ready to go now."

First Mate Leonard stopped and looked at her. "Oh no, you're not—"

"Leonard!" Captain Edward interrupted. "She can go."

Leonard sighed. "No, I didn't mean that, I meant she's not going alone. I'll go with her."

Ruth tried to hide her surprise—and confusion!—as she glanced over at Captain Edward. All of a sudden, the man who had enslaved her wanted to make sure she would be protected and not be taken by someone else? It seemed strange.

Captain Edward, too, didn't seem so sure of this unusual offer. It was a good idea, just odd to be suggested by Leonard. "I'll go too," Captain Edward offered.

Ruth led the way down the ramp and along the beach. As she limped just ahead of Captain Edward and First Mate Leonard, the morning breeze danced with the wisps of brown hair that had escaped her coif. She breathed in the cool ocean air. She looked down and watched the water sweep over her sand-dusted toes. She could almost hear herself singing "O the Deep, Deep Love of Jesus." It was just like that morning on the beach all those weeks ago, just before she'd ended up on the ship. And just like then, her heart was filled with warm content.

Things were increasingly familiar to Ruth as she neared the place she called home. She thought about all that had happened and all that she'd learned between now and when she had last been here.

At a spot known only to her, she turned and walked up the beach toward a cluster of run-down buildings. Not too much further, she stopped beside one of them.

"Well," she said, turning to Captain Edward and First Mate Leonard, "this is it!"

Captain Edward stared wide-eyed at the old, dark shack. The walls were sagging so badly that a good chunk of the roof had slid off. Holes marred what was left of the roof and walls, and the ground was dirty and wet and littered with trash.

He opened his mouth, but stopped. Like he had said, the choice was Ruth's. Yet how could he leave her to such a meager, unsafe place? He took a deep breath and waved. "Farewell, Ruth. Thank you for everything. I and the others will always be grateful for your pointing us to the Lord."

Ruth's eyes sparkled. "It was my pleasure." She glanced over at Leonard. He was watching silently with his usual serious scowl.

"Well..." sighed Captain Edward, "um, farewell." With that, he and Leonard began walking back.

"Farewell," echoed Ruth. She watched them as they left, then set her Bible on the ground and looked around her little place. She picked up her old, holey blanket and glanced up at the roof. It had provided her only shelter for the last two years. *God has been good to me in this little place,* she thought. *But He's been good to me in other places, too.*

It was another two hours later before the cargo was loaded and the ship's path plotted out. Not many words were spoken as the men went about their duties.

"The men and I are going to finish up some things in the village," Captain Edward said to Leonard. "Would you mind watching the ship while we're gone?"

Leonard gave him a confused look. He was surprised that Captain Edward was trusting him with such a job after how little he had trusted him regarding Ruth. "Aye, sir," he shrugged.

The others left, leaving Leonard by himself on the ship. Normally, Leonard walked around the ship when he was on watch duty. Not today. He had too much on mind. He'd been shouldering it and pushing it to the side, but now that he was alone, he wanted to figure out what it was that had been bothering him. He stood on the edge of the ship and put his hands on the railing.

"I snapped at her, but she was genuinely respectful to me. I hurt her, but she always wanted to help me. She nearly died trying to escape me; but later, when I needed help, she wouldn't let me escape her notice. I made her work hard, but she was willing to work even harder to help me. And in the end, she was ready to lay down her life for me! That's just so wrong!" Suddenly the little prickle of guilt in his conscience bit him deep. Leonard didn't let himself get upset about many things, but this was so disturbing he just couldn't help it.

"I just don't understand," Leonard sighed. "It seemed she forgave me, but that's impossible. Besides, even if she did, that's not good enough! I have to go back and fix it, but I can't. Must I hold this guilt forever?" Leonard's eyes started welling up, and his throat began burning. He tried to swallow it back and buried his head in his hands. Yet despite his best efforts, he couldn't help but cry. He'd never been so upset in his life. It felt like his pride, his confidence, everything he'd found his strength in, had suddenly come crashing down.

"She said she did it because God had forgiven her," he muttered. "But she said He could forgive me too." Leonard sighed. This was just too much to take.

"I'm too wretched of a man for God to care about me," he cried. "I've wronged her, and I've wronged other people. No one even knows some of the stuff I got into when I was younger. But she said he said God cares about all of us, no matter what we've done. He cared about the others. They've done wrong things too. I guess that means maybe I'm something to Him. God—"

Leonard took a deep breath. For the first time in his life, he prayed. "God, look. I don't know *what* You see in me, but I know You're real. I know You're out there. I have no idea how, but I believe You can clean up the mess I've made of my life…"

Unaware to Leonard, small footsteps neared the ship and began climbing up the ramp.

"Jesus…" Leonard continued praying. "I want to be free from this. I've had enough of it. I know it will mean rethinking everything in my life, but I'm going to find You. And I'm going to serve You. I believe everything Ruth said about You…" Leonard raised his hands in the air. "…and I'm going to serve You as Lord of my life from now on."

Instantly, it was like a switch flipped inside his chest. The guilt was lifted, and in its place was contentment and peace. A smile filled his face, and he heard someone dropping something behind him. He turned around to see Ruth with a knapsack at her feet.

She stood in shock, jaw dropped, with tears in her own eyes. She shook her head in disbelief.

"Are—are you—are you serious?" she stammered.

Leonard grinned, and he began to chuckle. Ruth's face lit up. "Oh, Leonard! I'm so happy for you!" she cheered. She bounded over to him and hugged his side. Leonard didn't mind. He knew what she meant. Leonard chuckle became laughter, and Ruth laughed along with her higher-pitched voice. "I've been praying for you so much!" Ruth exclaimed.

"Thank you," Leonard answered. "Thank you so much—for everything."

"I was just God's tool," replied Ruth.

"But it still took a lot to do what you had to do," Leonard pointed out. "So thank you."

Ruth's face glowed with a brilliant smile. "Hallelujah! God is so good!"

"Yes, He is." Leonard's face reflected her smile. Glancing around, he asked, "Why are you here?"

Ruth's eyes sparkled. "Can you help me with something?"

"Depends on what it is," answered Leonard with a twinkle in his eye.

Ruth glanced around, then explained her idea to Leonard.

Leonard grinned. "Are you sure you want to do that?"

"Yes, I'm sure!" Ruth exclaimed.

"Alright, then," Leonard agreed, nodding. "You have my permission."

Free

Not much later, the other men returned to the ship and prepared to leave. The ramp was raised, the anchor weighed, and the ship began to ebb its way from the harbor.

Charles went to the lookout, Augustus manned the rudder, and Sean directed the positioning of the sails. Captain Edward, though, sat for a moment on a barrel and looked out over the sea. It was the same barrel Ruth had sat on two weeks earlier — the night he had draped his coat around her.

"'The servant abideth not in the house for ever'," Captain Edward whispered to himself, swallowing hard. A lump caught in his throat, and his eyes burned with the beginnings of tears. "She didn't have to stay here," he reminded himself. "But, alas, I should've asked her to stay. She's a girl, a young disabled girl, out there surviving on her own! What were you thinking!" he demanded himself. "You could've taken care of her and provided her with things now she'll never have!" Captain Edward sighed. "I don't know what it's like to have a daughter, but it seems she came as close to that as anyone could." A tear ran down his cheek as he stared out over the endless ocean.

Of course, Captain Edward wasn't the only one thinking about Ruth. Everyone was. Breaking the gloomily silence, Stephan spoke for them all.

"You know, I never thought I'd say this, but I'm going to miss her. And it's not because of the food or the cleaning!" he chuckled.

"I know what you mean," agreed Augustus. "She just brought a whole atmosphere with her that's gone now."

Hector walked over and put a hand on Captain Edward's shoulder. Captain Edward took a deep breath and sighed as he continued staring at the horizon.

First Mate Leonard walked over, trying to hide a smile as he listened to the conversation.

"She sure did," Leonard said, agreeing with Augustus. "But I read her Bible."

At this, the other sailors turned toward him in surprise—even Captain Edward. They realized Leonard had a smile twitching on his face—a rare occurrence.

"Oh, good. That's great," smiled Alan.

"Yes," nodded Leonard. "And I understood why you all have changed since 'getting saved'. And I came to like it and want it myself. That's why…"

Leonard paused. The other sailors held their breath expectantly, hoping they knew what Leonard was about to say.

Leonard looked up, and with a big grin said, "…I've decided to make Jesus Lord of my life."

The sailors cheered! Charles threw his arms around Leonard's shoulders, and Alan patted his back.

"We're all…" Alessio paused abruptly. "What was it she called it?"

A distinctly high-pitched voice rang out across the deck. "Family!"

The sailors whipped around.

"RUTH!" Captain Edward gasped. "Wha—what are you doing here?"

Ruth burst into fits of laughter, leaving the sailors staring at her dumbfounded.

"Little miss stowaway," teased Alan when he came to himself.

"She had my permission," assured Leonard. Ruth shot him a playful glance that told everything.

Free

Stephan shook his head in astonishment and threw up his hands. "I should've known you were up to something by that smirk you were hiding!" he said to Leonard.

Leonard shrugged. "Her idea. I don't know how she managed to keep anyone from finding her."

"I hid in my room behind a stack of sacks," Ruth grinned. "My surprise worked!" Her eyes met Captain Edward's. He smiled, looking into her bright blue eyes. It was just like when they had met. Only now, instead of anxiety, their hearts were filled with warmth and happiness.

"What made you decided to come back?" Captain Edward asked.

Ruth beamed, but then changed to a more thoughtful tone. "Before we...met," she explained, "I asked God to give me a mission and a place to belong. And it seems..." she paused, and her face lit up. "It seems He has!"

The sailors cheered, and Captain Edward sighed with relief. Ruth's eyes sparkled, lingering as they disbanded. Hesitantly, she limped over to Captain Edward. They looked at each other for a moment, Ruth's eyes patient and trusting; his soft and gentle.

Captain Edward reached out a calloused hand as if to touch her hair, then drew it back. In one smooth motion, Ruth slid herself into Captain Edward's strong embrace. For a moment, Captain Edward stood awkwardly, glancing around at the sailors around him. They kindly pretended not to notice — even Alan, after Charles tapped his shoulder. Ruth pulled away and looked up at his uncertain face. Captain Edward relaxed and smiled. He picked her up and spun her in a circle, sending Ruth into laughter he couldn't resist joining.

As Captain Edward set her down, Ruth hugged him tightly. For a moment, she thought she was in the warm embrace of her own father. "Papa..." she began to say. But then she opened her eyes and remembered where she was.

Captain Edward's smile filled his face. "I don't mind if you call me that," he whispered. "I'll try to protect you and provide for you the same way your father would if he were here."

Ruth smiled. "You already have."

The sailors exchanged grins. Up in the rigging, one of the sailors began to sing:

"Amazing grace! How sweet the sound

That saved a wretch like me!

I once was lost, but now I'm found,

Was blind, but now I see..."

The other sailors joined in, and as their voices rose up, Captain Edward rubbed Ruth's shoulder. "Welcome home, Ruth," he whispered.

One short, ordinary girl—with a limp, too. Yet, God had used her to shine His light, sing His praises, and lead these sailors to a home in His love. And now, the Lord had provided her a new home as well. Her— just an ordinary girl who kept her eyes on an extraordinary God.

As the sailors began singing verse three, Captain Edward reached down to wipe tears off Ruth's face.

"Through many dangers, toils, and snares

I have already come.

Tis grace hath brought me safe thus far...

And grace will lead me home."

Free

Ruth smiled up into her new father's face. "His grace has led me home."

As Ruth stood in Captain Edward's shadow, she wondered what adventures lay in store. But of one thing she was certain: they would only continue to show her all the ways in which she was free.

> *For perhaps he was for this reason separated from you for a while, that you would have him back forever, no longer as a slave, but more than a slave, a beloved brother...both in the flesh and in the Lord.*
>
> *(Philemon 15-16 NASB)*

The End

Nautical Dictionary

Here is a dictionary of the sailing terminology that appears in the book. On a ship, there is a specific word or phrase for everything!

Afore – toward the front (of the ship)

Anchor's aweigh – the anchor has cleared the ocean floor

Anchor detail – the men in charge of stowing the anchor as the ship gets underway

Batten down the hatches – close the access doors to the lower decks

Binnacle list – a list of sailors who are currently unable to work because of illness

Boatswain (pronounced "bo-zin") – an experienced sailor in charge of the positioning of the sails and rigging

Bow – the front of a ship

Cross-staff – a navigation instrument used before the invention of   the sextant

Deduced reckoning – a method of calculating a ship's position based on speed, time, and distance

Down the hatch – head below deck

Fisherman's reef – An arrangement of the sails used when the wind is too strong to rig them as normal but not making any headway, or forward progress, is not an option

Forecastle – the raised deck area at the front of the ship

Galley – the kitchen

Hard over – to turn the rudder all the way in one direction

Hulking – of questionable seaworthiness

Luff – slack; i.e. "luff" sails

Mess room – the place where the sailors eat (It's often the same room as the galley, but on Captain Edward's ship, they are two different rooms.)

Midshipmen – ordinary sailors who sleep in the middle area of the ship (The officers' cabins are often in the stern.)

Port – to the left. To the right is referred to as "*starboard*".

She won't answer – the ship isn't responding

Stern – the back of a ship

Sterncastle – the raised deck area at the back of the ship

Try a different tack – change how you're doing things; try something else

Unfurl – unroll (used in reference to sails)

Wind-over-tide – when the wind and tide are going opposite directions, making it difficult for the ship to make headway

Yard – the rigging area

Free

The success of your favorite authors in is your hands!

If you have enjoyed this book or if it has made a difference in your life, please consider leaving a review on Amazon or Goodreads (or both!). Book reviews are one of the primary ways that new authors gain exposure and credibility. Will you support an author by leaving a book review today?

Careena Campbell

About the Author

Careena Campbell is a homeschool graduate living in Tulsa, Oklahoma. She's written stories ever since she was a little girl, with the hope of one day publishing her books. She wanted to provide youth like her with stories that were exciting, uplifting, and had a positive influence. This is the first title she has released.

When she's not creating stories, preparing for college, or working at a bookstore, Careena enjoys creating historical costumes, jamming to her favorite music, and spending time with her dad, mom, and brother.

To learn more about the story behind this book, see upcoming titles, or contact Careena, visit her author website at theanchoredwriter.com.

This page left intentionally blank.

Free

This page left intentionally blank.

This page left intentionally blank.

CPSIA information can be obtained
at www.ICGtesting.com
Printed in the USA
LVHW051141100421
684049LV00008B/122

9 781736 520802